FIXME

LISA M. CRONKHITE

FIX ME

Mendota Heights, Minnesota

First Edition
First Printing, 2017

Book design by Jake Nordby
Cover design by Jake Nordby
Cover images by Vladimir Galiak/Shutterstock; Anton Atanasov/Pexels

Flux, an imprint of North Star Editions, Inc.

This is a work of fiction. Names, characters, places, and incidents are either the product of the author's imagination or are used fictitiously, and any resemblance to actual persons living or dead, business establishments, events, or locales is entirely coincidental. Cover models used for illustrative purposes only and may not endorse or represent the book's subject.

Library of Congress Cataloging-in-Publication Data
Names: Cronkhite, Lisa M., author.
Title: Fix me / Lisa M. Cronkhite.
Description: First edition. | Minnesota : Mendota Heights, [2017]
Summary: "Teenager Pen Wryter tries to kick her addiction to Fix, an illegal drug featuring intense hallucinations, and solve the mystery of what happened to other Fix users who have disappeared"-- Provided by publisher.
Identifiers: LCCN 2017025640 (print) | LCCN 2017039280 (ebook) | ISBN 9781635830095 (hosted e-book) | ISBN 9781635830088 (pbk. : alk. paper)
Subjects: | CYAC: Drug addiction--Fiction. | Hallucinations and illusions--Fiction. | Missing persons--Fiction. | Depression, Mental--Fiction. | Suicide--Fiction. | Mystery and detective stories.
Classification: LCC PZ7.C88146 (ebook) | LCC PZ7.C88146 Fix 2017 (print) | DDC [Fic]--dc23
LC record available at https://lccn.loc.gov/2017025640

Flux
North Star Editions, Inc.
2297 Waters Drive
Mendota Heights, MN 55120
www.fluxnow.com

Printed in the United States of America

For my sweet darling Abba

CHAPTER ONE

"Just do it!" Rose demands, as we creep around the school grounds like two lost rats. "I swear Pen, I know you want to," she continues as we edge toward the graffiti-covered bleachers to find shelter.

Rose's hair flaps and waves like a brown flag in the high winds. She's shivering, trying not to drop the tiny round pill in her hand. I think if I look hard enough I'll be able to see my reflection in its slick black casing—like it's telling me to take it.

"Let me in, let me in," it's saying.

Rose crouches down, her bones protruding through her clothing. The drug is eating away at her. She almost loses control, rocking back and forth as if the repeated motion will speed up time. Her delicate skin has begun the transformation from its natural caramel color to a lighter shade of tan these days. Her jittery body is almost unbearable to watch. But Rose never seems bothered by the side effects.

I give her one hard look, like I am finally going to quit this time. I woke up this morning planning to quit. And now, here I am. Maybe just one more time?

I haven't seen Nate in days and I miss him terribly. The only reason I get high is to see him. He's the one good thing in my life since everything else is so screwed up. And he needs to know the truth. I need a chance to explain that I'm quitting.

"I'm so fucking serious, Pen. Mine's kickin' in right now, so make your mind up already." She pulls my left hand out and plunks the pill into my palm. It melts into the fine lines of my hand. Would it really hurt to take it just one more time? After overanalyzing and watching Rosario shiver, I chicken out about kicking the habit. I bring the pill to my mouth, popping it like candy. What the hell.

As the pill rests in the middle of my tongue, Rose tugs at my parka.

"Hurry up," she urges. The gel-like covering dissolves quickly and the liquid center begins to drip down the back of my throat. I could spit out the polluted shot at any moment, but Rose would have a fit if I waste any, so I swallow the sloshing juice and try to straighten out my nerves.

"There, that's better. Now I can see everything," she says, a Cheshire cat grin spread across her face, scanning the scene with her newly doped-up eyes. "Come on, let's go."

"Are you sure you wanna do this, Rose?" I ask her, hoping she'll change her mind and want to ditch again. I seriously can't face those jerks at school. Sneaking in high has its own risks. I know all the ways to get in and out of school undetected. But since Kelly Becker went missing a few weeks ago, the school's security has been tight. I can't afford to get caught.

"Don't worry," Rose tells me, widening her grin to an almost-believable smile. "Nothing's going to happen, I promise."

We race toward the school. Clearly, she's excited since she's now higher than a freaking kite. I suppose I would be too if I got all the attention that she gets at school. I'm not even sure why a pretty girl like Rosario Rodriguez would want to hang out with someone like me. She wouldn't be caught dead in the flannels and plain blue jeans that I wear. Everything Rose wears must have a famous designer name attached to it. And Rose has this long, lusty hair, while I keep mine shoulder length, changing colors each week. This week it's a bright red.

Rose laughs wickedly as we pick up speed across the football field to get to the front doors.

"This is a riot," she laughs. "You should see what I'm seeing."

Each person has their own unique experience while they're on Fix. I've never taken any other type of drug, but my friends who have experimented say that nothing really compares to it. Fix gives you some control over your hallucinations. When you trip on crack or meth, you have no control. Or so I hear. But on Fix, you can change how you see things. You can deepen the sky into a purple haze or tune in to your favorite music just by thinking about it. Yet, I know of no one that has an invisible friend like I have in Nate. And not many of my friends know about him, either.

We make it inside before the first bell rings. The Monster energy drink I had for breakfast comes up, fouling my mouth with sour ginseng aftertaste. I feel like I'm about to throw up, but I manage to hold it in. Not everything about being high on Fix is fun.

Rose and I begin to separate as I get close to my locker. "Keep your eyes open, Pen. Remember, don't fall asleep," she says, slowly walking away as I turn toward my locker.

"I can't. I won't," I tell her while cramming my backpack

into my locker. But apparently, I am talking to myself. When I swivel back around, she's already gone.

I slam the locker door shut, and it all kicks in. Suddenly, I can almost see inside my head—snippets of memories floating around like tiny dust particles. Little feathery fibers drift about, distracting me as I head to class. Once I clear them away, my senses rise like an ascending elevator. From the cafeteria, the smell of burnt meatloaf wafts in the air and the taste of soupy mashed potatoes lingers on my lips. The sounds of students walking through the halls vibrate in my bones. Conversations, both loud and quiet, bounce off the walls. Yet with the drug, I can easily tune them out.

I look down at my arms, watching them dangle and become numb. I'm literally floating to homeroom, yet in the sea of students that flood the halls, not a soul notices.

The light changes from the early Monday morning brilliance to a pale purple glow with a tinge of orange. And instead of the principal's announcements over the intercom, I tune my mind into an alternative station and glide through the halls like a ghost, drifting inside first period homeroom.

Nate begins to materialize in the corner of the room. Excitement and anxiety clash inside my body. The smell of raw metal lingers in the air. That's what Nate smells like.

Dark shadows in the shape of a slender young male appear like a dancing ribbon of smoke. I keep looking around to see if someone notices. No one does.

Then I lock eyes with my ex-boyfriend Walker. I'm paranoid and wonder if he knows what I'm up to. Walker always makes me feel guilty about Nate. Now he's eyeing me up from the front row. He thinks that with his icy-blue eyes and sexy hair he has power over me.

"Don't," he says, staring me down as I walk past him to my seat. "Remember what happened before . . . just don't do it."

"Shh," I whisper back. "Just leave me alone."

I wave Walker off as he gives me one last look of disapproval before glancing away.

Once I take my seat, Nate's dark shadows continue to solidify. His translucent skin swirls into a tan flesh color. I softly signal for him to wait. If I could just make time slow down, then I'd be ready to escape.

Nate's standing there, in the corner of the room—still, silent, waiting. The teacher scribbles on the whiteboard oblivious to the changes I'm seeing, as are all the students—everyone but Walker. His cautious eyes poison me with a look of dread. I can't help but think Walker's jealous of Nate. I don't know why. God, Nate isn't even real. Even though Walker does Fix, too, he still judges me for taking it. We've been friends forever, but ever since that night we first took Fix together, things haven't been the same.

Nate's long, wavy hair nestles around his porcelain face as black symbols etch themselves into the fine lines of his skin. They're the branded symbols that show he isn't real—a tattooing of sorts. And there always seems to be a new one every time we see each other. I wonder, for the first time, how much control I really have over him.

I raise my hand to be excused. The teacher nods and gives me a bathroom pass. I crawl out of the desk-chair and walk toward the door. From the corner of my eye, I see Nate trailing not far behind.

Once we get into the hall, he looks at me with loving

eyes, still waiting for my every command on what to do and where to go next.

"Come on, let's get out of here," I tell him, softly. "Just stay close and follow me."

CHAPTER TWO

Once we head outside, the cold stings my exposed skin. The temperature dropped big-time since Rose and I were out earlier this morning.

Nate clings tightly to my hand, trying to provide warmth to my body, but it's barely working. His nervous energy knocks my thoughts around. Am I making the right decision? How will he take the truth?

"Is everything alright, Penelope?" Nate asks.

"Yes," I say. "Just trust me."

Though, honestly, I don't trust myself. I don't trust myself to make this final decision for him. For us. But deep down, I know quitting is the only way. This has gone on long enough.

Nate and I walk hand in hand over the frost-covered football field. I want to take him to where this all started—the Tower. For almost a year, Fix has clouded my mind into one big, disorderly mess. Memories of me and Nate in the past jumble together with thoughts of the future, while the present just stands still. It's like a dream repeating over and over. This madness has got to stop.

The longer we stay here, the worse it will get. Plus, it isn't safe to be walking around with an imaginary person. I'd probably be hospitalized if anyone saw me talking to myself. I take Nate to the parking lot and head to my car.

"Hurry, we haven't got much time," I tell him.

"Please, Penelope, tell me what's wrong."

"Shh . . . Nate, I need to do this."

I nervously slide into the driver's seat and put the key into the ignition, revving up the engine. I try to stay positive and think of the things I *can* do. Like for instance, I can change the hue of the sky—or the sounds that I'm hearing. I can tune out things that are right in front of me or listen to a conversation in the distance. Sometimes though, I'm not sure if they're real or just in my head.

We pull out of the parking lot and drive away. The dusty autumn leaves float through the open windows. Crisp, crunchy fall flavors tickle my taste buds as if I just finished eating cornflakes without the milk. The earthy smells clog my nostrils and cause me to cough. All my five senses are more pronounced when I'm on Fix. That's one of the biggest attractions of the drug. But once it wears off, so does everything else. And the crashing side effect of coming down is like your brain hitting a brick wall at top speed. I'm not looking forward to the end of this high.

Instead, I focus on the here and now and my beautiful Nate. Right now, I've managed to keep the sky tinted purple. It always reminds me of my sister, Tabatha. Plus, it quells my worries. The dimly lit sun could almost pass as an off-color moon. Even though it's only ten in the morning, this change in light feels very real to me.

We finally get downtown to Al's Parking Lot. Nate's been oddly quiet this whole time. Fix only lasts about four hours, so we'll have to hurry. I wouldn't want to get stuck somewhere and not be able to get back home. When I'm off the drug, everything seems to go wrong.

We park my sister's Oldsmobile Cutlass—one of the

things I got when Tabatha passed away. After getting out, we walk straight for the Tower. The dilapidated building sticks out like a massive scar, sandwiched between two newer buildings. I glance at Nate every now and then, watching him as he looks up at all the tall structures. I'm afraid he knows what I'm about to do.

"Is everything okay?" Nate asks. I turn toward him, jiggling his hand, and tell him not to worry.

"This is the place, isn't it?" he asks, stopping in front of the Tower doors.

"Yes . . ." I want to say more but haven't the heart. My eyes travel upward to the very top, the place we first met.

"Are you sure you want to do this?"

"Yeah . . ."

We walk down the narrow, musty alleyway to get to the back of the building. I can't imagine what it's gonna be like to never see Nate again. But I also can't keep getting high. I know I love him. But that's messed up. He isn't real.

I try to focus on where we're headed. These days, the Tower is a rundown apartment complex full of junkies. Last year when I first started Fix the Tower wasn't so scary. Now a bunch of druggies live here. Most of them stay here to create their own world. But to normal people, it's a decrepit building that should be demolished.

We walk through the restricted construction area, crawling underneath plastic tarps and a cracked cement walkway. Some of the building's glass windows are shattered. At the very top of the structure looms an ever-present cloud. I don't know what it is—a rain cloud or fog or perhaps smoke, or just something of my own imagination. But it's there. And it just so happens to be where we're headed—the rooftop. The very place Tabatha fell to her death.

CHAPTER THREE

"It's never too late to change, Penny Girl," Tabatha always used to say to me. But my sister has no say in things now. Sometimes, I hate her so much I want to go where she is now just to slap her senseless.

Nate and I stand at the back of the building, freezing from the cold until he pries the door open. An even colder wave of air gusts past me as we step inside. Flickering fluorescent lights give an eerie glow to the walls. The halls are strangely quiet. I start to think no one's in the building until we hear soft echoes from the upper floors.

"Where to next, Penelope?" Nate gently asks. I shiver so hard I can't stop my body from vibrating. He stops in front of me, looks up, then comes close to give me his warmest embrace. His barely clothed body makes my skin prickle with goose bumps.

"Thank you," I manage to say through chattering teeth.

"My pleasure," he says. "Penelope, it will all be okay. I promise."

Once I warm up, Nate loosens his grip, pausing for a moment or two in the hallway.

"Feeling better?" he asks with a smile.

"Yes."

Honestly, I don't. The more time I spend with him, the less I want to quit Fix.

As I walk through the halls, my mind organizes, separating out each individual thought. The drug is trying to straighten out my brain, but it only makes things more confusing.

"Come on, Penelope, let's go somewhere safe," he urges.

Dread floods through me. No place here is safe. I should have never brought him to the Tower. He gives me a saddened look, like he knows I'm about to say something bad, so I tell him in a firm tone, "Let's keep moving."

He swings a door open and we both start up the steps. As we ascend, floor by floor, faint voices mingle in the stagnant air. Luckily, as we approach each level, no one bothers us. The whole time we're climbing the stairs, I'm thinking this dreamworld will end badly if I don't end it first. I have to be smart about this. I have to quit.

"Almost there, this way," he tells me.

How does he know where I want to take him? Is he on to me yet? Maybe he wants out of this madness, too.

"We're here," he says, standing by the rooftop entrance. He then turns around to look me in the eye. "Sure you're okay?"

"I'm not sure anymore." I look down at the cement floor and watch it spin. Before I can lose my balance, Nate grabs me so I don't fall down the stairs.

"Nothing's going to happen to you as long as I'm with you," I hear him say, yet his lips didn't move. Did he just say that? Man, am I hearing things? Why am I so unsure of everything?

"Huh?" I ask again. "What'd you say?"

Nate holds me close, cups my chilled face in his warm

hands and says, "My whole purpose is to keep you safe. Always remember that."

He opens the door and lets me walk out to the roof first, then then follows behind me. The cold, icy flooring is slick and hard to walk on.

"Be careful," he says. "I'm right here."

I look down for a while so I can ingest the beautiful words Nate has spoken to me, trying to win the tug-of-war in my mind. I'm not sure if it's Fix starting to wear off or if it's something else.

He holds me tight so I don't slip on the thin, black ice. The rooftop is covered with cracks as though I just might fall through into a deeper hell. Gray plumes of smoke loop upward from the chimneys. We walk through the foggy maze toward the dark brick edge.

"I want you to be okay," Nate says.

I put my hands up to his chiseled face to warm his stone-like skin.

"I know," I tell him, without having to explain much. "Just stay with me right now, okay?"

"I will. I will stay with you for as long as you need me," he says, holding me close. He gazes into my eyes and lets me see inside his soul. It's a vision of when we first met.

Staring into his silver eyes, he shows me the scene as if I'm watching a small TV screen. It's the night of the party in the Tower, when I first took Fix. I'm standing there—the same place I'm standing now at the edge of the building. I wanted to get away from the crowd that night so I went to the rooftop, leaving Rose, Walker, and my other friends back inside. My hair was longer then, a natural golden blonde, before I cut and dyed it. I'm wearing a small black cocktail dress, something you would never see me wear now. I'm crying . . . remembering Tabatha and when I lost her, the ache in my heart, the pain in my mind. All I kept thinking was why? Why did she do it?

"Please, Nate. You don't have to remind me," I tell him as I watch the scene inside his eyes.

"No, Penelope, you need to be reminded. I can't lose you."

As I continue gazing into his eyes, pictures form. He shows me on the ledge, my hair feverishly blowing in the wind. There I am, crouching down, holding on to the small brick slab at my feet. I remember the city below lit up like tiny stars in an underground sky. The downtown streets were in constant motion. Everything just kept going and going. There was no change, no difference in the world. Life went on without my sister. I figured life would go on without me, too.

My mother was already on her fourth boyfriend and didn't care about me. And my father drank himself into an early grave right after my sophomore year of high school. Things were already rocky with Walker.

Nate's eyes continue to play out the picture. I see myself stand up and lean over the edge.

I say to Nate, "I know what you're trying to tell me. Believe me, I'm not going to try to hurt myself like that again." It was the worst decision I ever made, trying to copy what Tabatha did.

I plead for Nate to stop, but he keeps showing me. His growing concern for me sends chills through my body. He knows something is wrong. But if he thinks I'm going to attempt suicide again, he's wrong. How am I going to tell him that I want to quit? That I'll never see him again?

"Just watch, you need to be reminded," he urges again. I've never heard him be quite that direct before. The vision in his eyes replays that scene. I'm right back there, at the ledge, looking down. And just when I teeter forward, warm arms wrap around my waist and pull me inward. When it happened a year ago, at first I thought it was Walker, but when I turned around and opened my eyes, there Nate was. He startled me. He was a stranger. It wasn't until later that I realized my subconscious created him because, even in my Fix-altered mind, I didn't really want to die.

"Nate please stop, I'm done. I'm done with all this!" I shout out. He looks at me in shock and begins to change.

CHAPTER FOUR

"Stay back," he warns, his silver eyes flaring into a bright Mediterranean blue. His muscles quiver as his tattoos begin to move, slithering around his neck and face.

Fear snaps me into a still photo. I can't move. I tell him to calm down. But it's probably not very effective since I'm freaking out, too.

"What's happening to you?" I ask, taking a step back, trying not to slip. Tears stream down his face. *Oh my God! What have I done?*

Warm green haze swirls in his irises. I realize he's charged up—hyper with energy in a way, and yet he's completely sad at the same time. The sky opens as threatening clouds roll in. Nate begins to rise; his feet no longer touch the ground. His eyes transform into two mood rings. I'm in awe. My first reaction is to run away, yet it is as if lead fills my bones. *This cannot be happening!*

I manage to creep backward, watching his pale skin transform into a pinker hue. He is beaming with light. *Dear God, what is he?*

"Nate, please calm down . . . you're scaring me."

He says nothing, rising up, just floating there.

Silence. Nothing but pure silence between us. The stunned feeling invades my thoughts like a plague. I don't know what to say. I don't understand. Nate has never looked any different. I'm afraid of how he looks now.

"Please tell me what to do. I don't know what you want from me."

"Nothing," he says in a firm voice.

My eyes widen in shock. My mind races in circles and back to the beginning again. Not sure of anything. I'm trembling and can't seem to shake it off. *Do I make a run for it?*

We are still like statues. His magnificent beauty ropes me in tight. I stare in shock as my thoughts stiffen.

"Tell me what to say . . . tell me what to do, Nate, please!"

And just then, as softly as ever, he whispers, "Do you love me?"

Speechless, my thoughts are trapped inside me. I do love him, but I've always found it to be a comforting companionship kind of love. Not romantic. Yet, now this is . . . this is so, God . . . I just don't understand. Am I in love with my own creation? Oh, God . . . or is he something else?

"Say something!" He pleads with me with his dimming eyes, and looks away as if he has lost something—me. I can tell that my hesitation is making him more concerned. The whole light inside of him fades.

"Please, Penelope, tell me the truth."

I look back into his eyes, not sure if I can. I just don't know anymore. Confusion has me tangled up inside.

The prolonged silence is slowly starting to kill him in some way. Warm salty tears of bewilderment travel down my face. I can't bear to see him like this. But I must be real here. I can't just fly away into whatever happily ever after. Can't stay on Fix forever. I don't want to live in this dreamlike state anymore. I have to quit. I have to say good-bye.

"Please, Nate. I'm sorry. I don't know! Please believe me!" I plead with him, shying away from my feelings.

"I'm afraid I don't. You can't even look at me anymore."

He begins to turn around and leisurely step away—farther and farther away.

"Nate, wait!" I scream out.

"It's over, Penelope. You made your decision," he says. His words are distant, traveling off into the wind.

"Nate, stop, don't! Come back to me, please!" I yell out again. "Wait, you don't understand." I race after him as he slowly descends off the ledge.

"Jesus Christ, Nate, why won't you listen to me?" I reach into the foggy air. I close my eyes, for only a split moment in time and when I open them, he is gone.

Oh no! What time is it? I gotta get outta here!

The drug wears off, crashing me into reality. It isn't safe. I'm all alone on the rooftop of the Tower. Some druggie can come out and rob me, or worse.

I look over the ledge to see any signs of Nate, but he just vanished into thin air.

Okay, okay . . . keep it together.

I swivel back around and rush to the exit door. Gradually, the walls change from the normal white they used to be to a chipped black. It's even worse than the way I saw it when I was stoned. I reach into my pocket for my phone to see what time it is—10:45 in the morning. *Damn!* I've missed too much school already. I wonder if they've called my mom yet.

I race down the stairs, taking a few deep breaths along the way. My heart is beating a million miles per minute.

My hands sweat as I try to hold onto the railing, but I can't get a good grip. *Get a grip!*

I trip on the last stair, hitting the ground hard. My exhausted body drops instantly against the hard floor. I struggle to get up. The back of my head is bleeding. *Why do I put myself through this?*

I manage to get up and walk to the back exit on the main floor. Once I swing the door open the bright afternoon light hits me like a swinging baseball bat to my face. Dark watery liquid rushes up my throat and spews out like a black fountain. It's like the liquid in Fix. It's almost as if it multiplies and creates all this extra fluid inside me. Then piercing cramps contract inside my abdomen, causing me to buckle in pain. *Damn!* This happens nearly every time the drug stops working. *Jesus Christ, help me keep it together.* After the pain in my stomach subsides, starvation carves a hole in my belly.

I grope my hands along the brick wall of the building for support and find a shady spot in the alley. I look around and see my car isn't there. *What the hell? Great. As if things couldn't get any worse. Crap, now what?*

My head pounds as if a drummer from a rock band went haywire in my skull. I check the back of my head again. *Ok, good. The bleeding's stopped.* I pull out my phone and dial Rose. It takes three rings before she answers.

"Hey, Pen, what's up?" she says to me, smacking gum over the phone.

"Rose, you have to help me. I'm stranded by the Tower."

"The Tower? Shit, girl, what possessed you to go there?" she asks, still popping her gum.

"Just get Clay to pick me up. I'm hurt pretty bad."

"What happened to you? Don't tell me. This had some-thing to do with that Nate thing, right?"

"Look, will you just get your boyfriend to pick me up?" I press on my head again to double-check for clotted blood.

"Okay, okay. Relax, I'll do it."

"Good."

I press end on the call, huddle behind the rotted-out dumpster, and wait for Clay's pick-up truck to come.

I'm in shock over what happened. I need to tell Nate how I feel and how much he means to me. It can't end like this. All I can think about, sitting here crouched up, is getting high again.

CHAPTER FIVE

After an hour or so I'm still waiting, with blood-caked hair and feeling weak, when Clay's truck pulls into the alleyway. Once I crawl myself up off the damp brick wall, I wait until Clay gradually creeps the truck closer. He gives me a big wave from out of the open window to let me know he sees me. I give a small wave back, trying not to lift my bruised arm too much. Clay seems excited that he spotted me. Maybe he was worried he wouldn't find me.

As Clay focuses his big black eyes on the potholes, I glance over to the passenger side. I can recognize that shaggy jet black hair anywhere. Walker. And with his steel-blue eyes locked onto mine, I can tell he's ticked off at me—as always. If I had any money, I would bet all of it that he's upset I ditched school and did something dangerous again. *I so do not want to hear this right now.*

Once Clay's close enough, I stumble to the truck and cram myself in the backseat. *Okay, deep breath, Pen, just keep it cool. This car ride should sure be fun . . . oh, man.*

Right away Walker barks at me like some annoying dog.

"What the hell made you come all the way out here?" Walker spits out. "What's the matter with you? Wanna end up like that one girl?" He turns around to examine me with his "I see everything" eyes. I try not to let it bother me, though I want to scream out, "It's none of your fucking business what

I do, so fuck off!" Why is he even bringing Kelly Becker up now? For all we know, she could just be a runaway. Sure, she was a "good girl." But those are exactly the type of girls with dark secrets.

Instead of blowing up in his face, I keep it cool. It isn't worth getting into another endless argument.

"Oh, wait, let me guess. You were all Fixed up and with Mr. Pretend again, right?"

"Leave her alone," Clay snaps with his deep voice as he pulls the truck back onto the main street. "Are you okay back there, Pen? You look a little banged up."

"Did your make-believe boyfriend invent some new punches on you?" Walker lashes out more word venom.

"Man, will you ever stop raggin' on her?" Clay whips back at him, while turning onto a Lake Shore Drive entrance ramp. "I swear, jealousy *is* your weakness, don't you realize that?"

"Just shut up and drive. What do you know anyway?" Walker snaps.

But Walker's wrong to be jealous. It's not like that with Nate. We're friends.

"Just quit it, both of you," I bark. I slink back down and try to get more comfortable. My aching head pounds with continuous thumps as if someone's banging the back of my head with a hammer. And I can't seem to get the last image of Nate out of my mind, which hurts even more than the pounding. I need to explain myself to him. And the worst part of this whole scenario is that I lost Tabatha's car.

"So, you gonna tell us what happened to you or what?" Clay asks again, clenching his lean, dark hands on the wheel.

"I fell down the stairs," I tell them. Total silence infects both of them. The fierce whipping wind from their open windows beats me down with cold air. More silence as Clay turns onto the St. Louis ramp.

"Well, you shouldn't have been out there," Walker says.

"Listen, I don't wanna talk about it anymore. Can we just drop it? Please? And roll the windows up while you're at it, will ya? I'm freezin' my ass off back here."

"You shoulda told someone where you were going. That's all I have to say about it," Clay adds as he rolls up his window. Walker already has his closed—and his mouth is finally closed, too.

"Are you sure you're okay back there, Pen? I can take you to the hospital or something."

"Thanks, Clay, but I'll be okay. Just stop worrying." I pause for a minute or two. I turn and look in Walker's direction. "Shouldn't you be in fifth period right now?"

"So what?" Walker asks.

"So why did you come with Clay?"

"God, you don't know, do you?" He looks at me in disgust.

"What? What am I supposed to know?"

"Just forget it. It's useless talking to you anyway."

"Walker, come on. I just feel like total crap. You guys are both seriously giving me a headache big time." I slump back again and try to focus on the tall buildings, but it's not working.

"Well if it wasn't for you calling, crying to Rose that you needed a ride, we all wouldn't be here right now, would we?" Walker snaps.

"Did I bother you for a ride? No!"

Clay chimes in. "Just quit it, okay? He's here because I

needed his help. The truck died out again, so I called him. Walker got Brian's car from his place and gave me a jump."

My heart suddenly sinks into the soles of my shoes. I completely forgot how unreliable Clay's car can be.

"You used Brian's car for that?" I totally feel like the dickhead now. Walker would never touch his brother's car unless it was truly an emergency. "I'm sorry . . . I didn't know."

"It's fine." Walker says, taking a deep breath. "That shit-head will never find out, anyway. And even if Brian did, what is he gonna do that he hasn't done to me before?"

"Walker, I didn't—"

"It's okay," Walker cuts in before I could finish. "Seriously, don't worry about it. You're okay, and that's all that matters right now."

I'm not sure why Walker's so concerned about my safety today. Now, I'm worried about his. Flashes in my mind bring me back to that horrible fight Walker and Brian had. He beat Walker so bad, Walker ended up in the hospital. I would be heartbroken if he got hurt like that again. And just because of me? Sure, Walker's a big jerk sometimes, but no one deserves to be treated like that.

Clay turns on the radio, cutting off the silence. I curl up with a junky old blanket rolled up in the backseat and try, *try* to relax. Again, my mind goes back to Nate. I'm dying to take Fix again, just to fix this mess between us.

We pull up to my house just before one o'clock. Clay zooms into the driveway and stops the car outside the backyard gate.

"Damn, Clay, can you get any closer?" I joke. Walker gets

out first, then Clay, as I'm balled up in the backseat. Before I get out, images of Nate pop into my head again. I can't get over how beautiful he looked—those continually changing eyes, that tan skin, muscles pumping underneath his lifelike tattoos. That inviting warmth nestling inside me, I miss it. I miss him. I wonder now more than ever if he's still here in some way, even without Fix. Then reality sets in, my head continues to pound, and I remind myself of how careless I was with Tabatha's car. I can't believe it's gone. I hope it wasn't stolen. Maybe just towed.

"Here, let me help you out," Walker says, opening the door and folding the front seat down so I can get out. He takes my hand, firmly gripping it so I don't slip on the thin sheet of black ice covering the driveway. The October temperature feels like the dead of winter.

"Watch out." Walker points to a small, icy puddle.

He helps me up the thick cement walkway after opening the gate and guides me across the patio to the back door.

"Thanks, Walker, you know you don't—"

"What? I don't have to help you? Come on, Pen, I can tell you're in pain."

I look down, not really knowing what to say next. Walker hasn't been this nice to me in a long time.

"Look, you guys. I gotta head out. Rose will have a fit if I'm not there to pick her up at lunch," Clay yells out, hopping back into his truck as Walker and I stand by the back door.

"That's fine. I got this," Walker yells back.

Clay revs up the engine and backs the truck down the driveway.

"You got what?" I ask, giving him a dirty look. "So, you think you have to babysit me now?" He gives me a sexy smile like he's got something more in mind. I've seen that look before. "Listen, you don't hafta stick around for me. I can manage," I urge again.

"Penelope, I don't know exactly what happened to you, whether you actually fell down the stairs or not. But I can tell when you're hurt bad."

"I'll be totally fine, really." I rummage in my pockets for my keys. "Ouch!" I bump my elbow on the opened screen door. When I reach out for my keys, they drop down into a slushy puddle. "Shit."

"I got it." Walker picks up the keys.

"Fine, I'm not going to argue with you right now."

"Good, don't." He smiles again as he hands me the keys. I turn around and unlock the door.

"Pen!"

"What?"

"Your head, it's bleeding."

"What? Not again." I raise my hand up to see if I opened the wound somehow, but no blood. "Oh, yeah, it was bleeding earlier. I think it clotted up now, though."

We look at each other for an awkward moment as my heart races. I haven't been alone with him in God only knows how long. Flashes of intimate times together overtake my mind. My cheeks begin to flare up.

"Umm, I think I got it from here. Thanks again." I look around the empty house and step inside. My mom must be on her shift at the bank.

"Please, Pen. Let me help you. I want to make sure you get some rest. Last thing I need is you falling again. Just until you get to bed, and I promise, I'm outta here after that." The roguish grin spreading across his face has me thinking he may have other intentions. With one look, I make him realize that I am suspicious.

"You think I'm going to make a move on you in your condition?" he says.

"Walker, you think you know everything. It isn't that." I look away before he figures out he's right. I can never seem to get away with lying to him.

"Come on, you're halfway there."

"Halfway where?" I ask.

"Halfway to your bed, so I can . . ." he kiddingly says, but I give him a good slap on the arm before he could finish.

"Just stop playin' around. My head hurts too much to laugh."

"So?"

"Fine, I guess. But don't mess with me, or I'll—"

"Yeah, yeah, I've heard it all before."

I give him a genuine smile to let him know I really do appreciate what he's doing for me.

He waits for me to close the back door before he takes his coat off.

"Come on, Penelope. Let's get you cleaned up."

CHAPTER SIX

"Let me see it!" Walker pleads through the bathroom door.

"No! I told you, I'll be fine. Let me handle it," I yell back.

"Please, Penelope, let me help." I cave to his sorrowful pleas and open the door.

"Fine! Look! Look at my ugly head! Happy now?" Why he's being this persistent about seeing my head injury is beyond me. It's not like I'm unconscious or it's spurting blood all over the place. This, I can handle.

He slowly approaches me and begins to softly pick through my hair like a chimpanzee. It couldn't be more uncomfortable.

"See! It's fine, now will you quit it?" I buck a little as he touches the sore spot. "Ouch! Watch it!"

He gets a washcloth from the linen closet and runs it under warm water.

"Just hold still," he instructs. "I just want to make sure you don't need stitches."

Walker of all people would know that difference. He's had so many stitches, you would think he's Frankenstein.

He gently presses my head down as he towers over me, examining the wound further. After he dampens the rag, he dabs my head.

"Well, from what I see, it's not that deep," he says, softly patting my wound. There's an awkward silence between us for a while. As I stare at the blue floor mats, my mind wanders back to the time I did the same thing for him. Brian had gone off on him for something so minuscule I can't even remember what it was. I always told Walker to relax and blow him off when he got like that, but he just couldn't. He grabbed Brian by the neck and swung with his left arm, punching him smack square in the jaw. Then, when Walker turned his back, Brian picked up an empty beer bottle and shattered it across the back of Walker's head. I'll never forget how gross it was to pick all the glass out of Walker's bloody hair.

"I'm not hurting you, am I?" he asks, standing close to me.

"No, you're good. Ooh, it just stings."

I watch his facial expressions in the mirror, diligently making sure the wound is clean. I try not to stare, but it's just too hard sometimes. Walker has always been a beautiful guy. His mesmerizing light-blue eyes peek out from underneath his dark, wispy bangs. If I stare into them long enough, I'll feel weak in the knees, like I had a few too many.

He looks up at me through the mirror's reflection and smiles. "I think you'll be okay, Pen. It's sealed up good." He swivels me around to give me a good look and brushes my hair away from my face.

My heart begins to beat a bit faster. This is awkward. He looks at me and smiles. "You know, Pen, I miss this."

I'm not sure what he misses. Cleaning each other's wounds? Being together? I don't know. He seems so mad at me most of the time. What is he thinking? Confusion keeps me from saying anything.

He moves in closer. We're almost touching faces now as he cradles my head in his hands.

"I miss you, Pen," he whispers. He tilts my head up toward his face and moves in, but I jerk back.

"Wait, I don't think we—" I pause mid-sentence, suddenly thinking of Nate, like I'm betraying him somehow.

Walker freezes in surprise, giving me a wide-eyed look. He backs away, shrugging his shoulders in disgust. It's obvious he thought I'd react differently.

"You know, I just don't get you anymore, Pen."

And neither do I, I want to say. But I don't think what I say is going to change things. I say something anyway. "Listen, I didn't mean to—"

"Just forget it, I'm outta here." He turns and leaves out the front door.

I'm stupefied. *What the hell? He told me he wasn't going to make a move.* I look in the mirror again, staring at my blue eyes and freckled face, confused. I check behind me, picturing him standing there. Suddenly, a burst of hurt floods my mind, filling my eyes with tears.

I take a few deep breaths, hoping to calm down, but I continue to think of Walker. I wonder how upset he is right now. It's not the first time he's been mad at me. How's it he can make me feel so bad?

It makes me think about the night before we broke up for good. I went to Justin's house to see if Walker was there—to talk things over, to tell him how sorry I was for missing our date that afternoon. It wasn't like I was blowing him off or anything. I just lost track of time.

Justin was sweet enough to invite me in and listen to my rant about Walker, even though I don't think he cared.

I remember he was hugging me and letting me cry on his shoulder. But when Walker arrived looking for me, he took it the wrong way. He thought we were messing around. He blew up yet again and that's when we broke it off—for good. I've kept a wall up between us from that point on.

I mope around, feeling like a scumball, so I decide to take a shower. Maybe it will help calm my frustration, and it will definitely get the blood out of my hair.

I bend down and turn the knob, letting the water run. Holding my hand out underneath the steaming waterfall, I lift the lever for the showerhead and step in.

Luckily, I don't have many bruises from the fall—just one on my knee, a small one on my left elbow, and the one on my head. I situate the mirrors on the wall just outside the shower and try to examine it more closely, but it's too hard from this angle. I should stop worrying about it. Walker did say it sealed up pretty good.

My body relaxes in the warm steam. I could collapse right here. I don't though. Instead, I just stand, letting the hot water spray my face. As I close my eyes, flashes of those ever-changing eyes appear.

Nate was nothing but wonderful to me. He was a dream, my endless companion. Was it all just a dream? Another hallucination from Fix? When I was little, I always imagined having a beautiful being protect me, like an angel. Could that have been Nate all along? I don't understand it. It's been nearly a year and Nate has never been upset with me before. He's always agreed with everything I said or did. In the beginning, I hated it—how he mirrored my every emotion—but I grew to accept it. I never thought it would change. How could it? Well, I was wrong—way wrong.

As I turn the water off and wrap myself in a towel, I make a promise to myself to find out all I can about this drug. How stupid could I be to take it and not fully know the consequences? To be honest, I didn't even think it could hurt me. I mean, the drug was originally made for people with depression, like Tabatha.

When Tabatha was taking it, she seemed to be fine. But, obviously, she wasn't. I still don't understand why she decided to kill herself. What was tormenting her to the point that she decided to end her life like that? And why didn't she come to me for help?

When I walk upstairs and into my room to change, I pass Tabatha's old room. Automatically, I make a U-turn and go in. It's all cleaned up now. Cleaned of her clothes, cleaned of her books, cleaned of her. And all I have is her urn to prove that she was ever here. Except for a few pictures on her dresser, her room is all I have left of her. There's a picture of her at five years old. Before I was born.

Many people said we looked a lot alike. But honestly, no one ever compared to Tabatha. Her long, golden locks always bounced upon her shoulders and her marble-blue eyes were translucent, almost like a cat's. I swear, she was a cat in another life, too—so playful, fun, and full of energy when she was young. It was just those last few years that remain a fog to me.

I look at her pictures, staring at my favorite one with just the two of us, standing side by side along the oceanside in Daytona Beach. It was on one of our family vacations, when all four of us were content. I'll never forget what she said. "See the purple sky, Penny?" she asked me, pointing to the setting sun. "I'm the purple . . . and just below that you're the pink." She was always poetic like that. Some things I didn't understand. Some things I still don't understand. But I can't let them destroy me like they destroyed her.

By the time I get myself together and walk the mile to school, it's already sixth period. I make it to my geometry class on time, but I can't pay attention to anything. I jiggle my leg under the desk and clutch my aching head. Somehow, I make it through. I head to the girls' bathroom just before the bell rings to end class. I want to try to text Clay. I'm hoping he'll take me back to Al's Parking Lot to see if we can find Tabatha's car.

I brush pass Candace and her clan of deadheads, smacking gum and laughing near the water fountain, and slide inside the girls' bathroom. *Good, it's empty.*

After taking a swift scan around, I head inside the large handicapped stall in the corner. I lock the door shut and hang my backpack on the hook. Moving to the farthest corner of the stall, I fumble with my phone. I'm having a hard time concentrating as my thoughts scatter.

I feel like I'm zoning out a little until a group of girls come in and snap me back to reality. Their mindless chatter annoys me. From their voices, I can tell its Candace and her clay dolls, Brandy and Emma.

"Haha, I know, and she's like so freakish, isn't she?" Candace says to them. Brandy's giant hairdo almost blocks my view through the tiny opening at the side of the stall door, as poor little "I'll do anything for you guys" Emma stands on the other side.

"I don't even know what he sees in her," Brandy adds, glancing in the mirror to make sure her hair is still standing ten inches above her. *Doesn't she realize no one wears their hair like that anymore?*

"Yeah, she's so damn ugly, anyways," Candace snickers. I have a feeling I know just who they are talking about.

"Do you think they're going to find Kelly?" Emma desperately tries to change the subject but Candace and Brandy ignore her. Candace wouldn't care if Kelly Becker was brutally murdered.

Candace waves Emma off. "Who cares?"

Clearly, they don't realize they are not alone. Typical deadheads—stupid as always. But I am cautious enough that they don't catch on to me. I cram myself a little tighter in the corner.

"It's only a matter of time. What I'm doing is working. I'm pretty sure Walker's over *that thing* anyways."

Oh, man! I knew they were talking about me. She's after Walker? Miss Bombshell Candace Roman with her perfect blonde hair and her perfect fake boobs has every guy at school drooling, but Walker? Why him? He isn't the type she'd go for. Walker's real. Candace isn't.

"Besides, doesn't Penelope have an imaginary boyfriend now?" Brandy snickers, playing with her hair.

The hair on the back of my neck stands up. *Has Rose been talking about me? Telling people about Nate?*

"That's cause she's a drugged-up FREAK!"

They all laugh. *Great. I'm glad my life is so hilarious.*

"Come on, back to the show," Candace kids around as she leads the girls out.

What the hell? Candace could have anyone, but she has to target Walker. Why? I don't see Walker being interested in a girl like her. Maybe that's what interests Candace the most—the challenge of getting what she can't have.

For second I just stare at the chipped paint on the stall door. I cannot remember why I'm in the bathroom. I notice my phone in my hands. *Oh right. Clay. The car.*

I keep scrolling through my contacts, but I can't find his name. I know it's the aftereffects of Fix messing with me—making simple tasks stupidly difficult. *Screw this.*

I text Rose.

Can you give me Clay's number again?
Sure thing, hold on.

The last period bell rings, but it doesn't matter if I'm late for my final class.

Here it is, babe. Rose texts me back with Clay's number.

Thanks, lady, talk to you later, I respond.

Oh, yeah, party at my house later. Getting a Fix circle together. You better be up for it tonight!

I want to see Nate again. But a Fix circle? Those can really mess you up.

But Rose is my main Fix supplier. If I don't get high with her, I'm probably not getting high at all. Everyone knows she's way into Fix. She got kicked off the gymnastics team last year because she was too messed up to perform. And, yet she's still using.

I turn off my phone and head out of the bathroom.

The halls are as empty as a scene in some nighttime slasher movie. But it's the middle of a bright and sunny afternoon, warm rays shedding light through the giant floor-to-ceiling windows. And I'm not quite alone. Jilly, the hall monitor, is at the corner end of the hall.

"Do you have a hall pass, Pen?" she asks as I approach her. I'm not surprised. Jilly, the valedictorian and the head of every club, is in charge of the west wing of the school, too.

"Actually, no I don't. I'm sorry."

"That's okay. I'll write you up one," she says, sliding her thick-rimmed glasses back up her long, sloping nose. "Hold on a sec." She takes a seat at her desk, rips off a piece of pink paper, scribbles something down, and then hands it to me.

"Thanks, Clay. I appreciate it." I grab the slip.

Jilly's eyebrows arch, and she gives me a half-confused, half-annoyed look. Only then do I realize that I just called her the wrong name.

"Uh, sorry, Jilly," I mumble as I walk away. But my stomach is all in knots. What is Fix doing to me?

Right then and there I decide enough is enough. I need more information.

I turn left to head up the stairs. With my pink hall pass flapping in one hand and my backpack in the other, I bounce up to the second-floor landing and head straight into the library. It sucks I don't own a computer. And since my mom has a limited data plan, it's too frustrating to look on my phone. But I can be old-school and use the library.

I want to know what Fix is really doing to my body. I know Rose suffers from some side effects, too. God only knows how many other potential side effects Fix has. What else am I in for if I don't quit?

I head straight to the computers, but I am stopped by Miss Liddy, the school librarian.

"Excuse me, there," she says, pointing in my direction. "Can I see a note from your teacher?"

I walk toward the front desk and rummage through my backpack, pretending to look for it.

"Oh, I'm so sorry Miss Liddy, I must have misplaced it," I tell her, hoping she'll let me go.

"Okay, I'll let you use the library this time," she says, sifting through some papers. "But you'll need a permission slip from your teacher next time. Here," she hands me a form. "Please fill this out and have it back to me by tomorrow."

"Thank you, Miss Liddy. I really appreciate this." I take the slip and stuff it in my backpack.

I make a beeline for an empty table to set my stuff down. I spot one near the windows, place my things on it, and head over to the computer lab. There are about a dozen computers and only three or four other students using them. *Good.* I wouldn't want to fight for one.

After picking one nearest to the wall, I plop down and sign in, opening Google.

I enter "fix" into the search bar and instantly a million links of the wrong thing pop up. *Urgh! God, stupid, that's not how it's spelled.* As I play around with the spelling, I finally open a few interesting links.

Phixeedifore, the New High, one of them says. So, I click on it.

Phixeedifore, commonly called "Fix," was an antidepressant and mood-stabilizing drug used primarily in the treatment of clinical depression and bipolar disorder. It was FDA approved on June 18, 2015, after several successful test studies. Yet when publicly administered to patients in late 2015 through early 2017, the drug was recalled due to a severe rash of fatal side effects, totaling more than 200 estimated deaths in the United States.

Patients complained of a plethora of symptoms, including constant vomiting, severe allergic reactions, blood in their stool or urine, and bleeding from the eyes, nose, and mouth. Common side effects include delusions of grandeur, rigorous hallucinations, and suicidal thoughts. In some very rare cases, patients have reported reoccurring visions of unknown people. No one has been able to explain their visions. Three such cases were reported between November 2016 and February 2017. All three patients committed suicide shortly after reporting their hallucinations. Because Fix has lasting effects and can remain in the bloodstream for up to eight weeks, such visions may still occur in patients after the dosage has long been discontinued.

In late April 2017, Congress passed a law, prohibiting Phixeedifore from distribution. It has now become one of the most popular illegal drugs in the United States to date.

Oh my God! Reoccurring visions of unknown people? Nate! And lasting effects?

A migraine threatens to take over the front of my forehead. I close my eyes to stop reading any more of the neon screen. I bow my head down as if unable to hold up the heaviness that's filling my mind, but then I will myself to read further.

I go back to the Google search bar and try to find more articles on those three rare cases. One link reads *Michigan Girl Commits Suicide Because of Fix*, so I click that and start reading: *Wendy Newman had a normal life. She was captain*

of the volleyball squad and had straight A's all throughout
high school. But when she fell into the wrong crowd, she
started experimenting with drugs. That's when she got hooked
on "Fix."

I look up and realize her story sounds like mine. I used to have a normal life before. Ever since I started hanging around Rose, after Tabatha died, I just didn't care anymore. That's why taking Fix didn't seem like a big deal to me. I wonder how many more girls out there are like that. I read on.

After developing hallucinations of a young girl, Wendy
tried to quit Fix. Yet reports from her mother and sister say
Wendy was still having adverse side effects even after the
drug was discontinued. Wendy then took drastic measures
to finally break free from Fix, and she slit her wrists in the
Newman's lakehouse.

She developed hallucinations of someone, too. Just like I have with Nate. Somehow, I find that a relief. Like I'm not the only one to go through this. And then she . . . killed herself?

I'm so frazzled that within seconds warm liquid rushes my nostrils. I sniffle and try to trap the mucus from running down further. *Great! I'm catching a cold now? It totally figures. Okay, okay, calm down. Let's just rationalize this.* Maybe it was just a rare case. Maybe it won't be like that for me. I certainly don't feel suicidal. I want to read more, but a wave of dizziness overcomes me, causing silvery spots to appear in front of me. And I'm scared to find out what I'll read next.

The runny feeling in my nose doesn't stop. Then suddenly, ooze drips down the back of my throat and into my mouth. *Gross!* When I smack my lips together, holding my hands up to my face, I realize the sweet, salty ooze isn't snot. *Oh, no! This can't be happening!* When I look down into the palm of my hand, I see red—red on my fingers, red on my sleeve, and red on my shirt. And I'm sure there's red all over my face, too. I try to contain the blood with a piece of paper and crumple it to my nose. *For Christ's sake, and I just read about the side effects and now I'm getting them?*

The final bell rings and no one notices my bloody waterfall, thank God. I gather my things, cup my nose, and head out.

CHAPTER EIGHT

I zip up my coat and put my hood on as the wind picks up. Rose asked Clay to give me a ride home after school, but I'd rather walk—try to collect my thoughts and think of ways out of this mess.

My nose stopped bleeding. I cleaned up before I left school, but there's crust in my nostrils, making it hard to breathe. I was surprised at first, but then remembered Walker complaining of nose bleeds from Fix before, so I'm not getting all twisted out of shape over it. I think there's a small sore in my nose now. I can't stop twitching my nose while I walk. It's a few hours before dusk and already darkness covers the sky in a curtain of navy blue. Some people already have Halloween lights and decorations up. I remember the last time I went trick-or-treating. I remember all the times Tabatha took me. I'll never forget when she got her first job at sixteen at Kmart. I was eleven at the time and still into Halloween. She bought me a costume with her first paycheck. It was a pink princess dress and, although my heart sunk because I wasn't into that stuff anymore, Tabatha's happiness was contagious, so I wore it for her anyway. You couldn't help but feel the same way when around her.

After she got her license and saved up enough money from her Kmart job she bought the Oldsmobile. *God! I still can't believe I screwed up so badly—lost her car and everything.*

As I cross Kilpatrick and head farther into the neighborhood, I reach into my pocket for my phone and dial 4-1-1 to get the number to Al's Parking Lot. Maybe if I talk to Al, I'll find out what happened to Tabatha's car. After three rings, his answering machine picks up. *Hi there, you've reached Al's, a place to park your car. We are not able to come to the phone right now but if you leave your name and n—.* I press end before it finishes. I think if Clay takes me, I'll be able to get some answers.

I rotate the phone in my hand as if I'm lathering up a bar of soap, debating on whether to call Clay or not. Going back to Rose's text, I use that to dial his number. He picks up right away.

"Yo, who dis?"

"Clay? It's Pen."

"Oh, hey girl, what you need?"

Poor Clay thinks that every time I call him it's because I need something from him. Then again, he's right.

"You think you can drive me up to Al's tomorrow sometime?"

"Maybe, why?"

"Tabatha's car. I need to find out what happened to it."

"Oh, yeah. That's right."

"So, can you?"

"I'll let you know later. You coming tonight?"

"Oh, to Rose's? Umm . . . I guess." I'm not looking forward to the Fix party tonight, but it's my chance to maybe see Nate again. If I can just see him one more time, try to explain, then I promise myself I'll quit for good. *Hopefully.*

"Cool, see you later, then," he says. He pauses for a minute. "So, you need anything else? Everything okay with you?"

"Yeah, yeah, I'm good. See you later."

I end the call, thinking to myself, *you liar, you're far from "good."* I don't want to lay around and go into la-la land with them tonight. But Nate. Panic stirs inside me at the thought that I might not see Nate again. Even if I did tell him how I feel, would it make a difference? I mean, come on, what would happen to us in the long run? We live happily ever after and have pretend babies? Christ, what is he thinking?

That's just it. I don't know what he is thinking. I don't know if he can think. All this time, I thought he mimicked my feelings. But this morning on the rooftop, he seemed to have feelings of his own. Guess I just was too stupid to realize it earlier.

It's only 4:35 and already the streetlights are going on. I'm not satisfied. I feel like I need to call someone else. I'm lonely. I really can't call Rose and tell her how I feel. I mean, she's an okay friend and all, but sometimes I just don't trust her. All she cares about is getting high. I can't call Walker either because he'll read into things too much.

I look at my phone again, scrolling up and down my contact list as I walk. There's all these names of people, half of whom I don't even talk to anymore. Kim, Trina, Dan, Marty, Matt, people I have gone to school with, hung out with on and off, yet I couldn't care less about. And I'm sure they feel the same. I go through all the names until I come to the one and only that makes me stop. *That's a blast from the past. Would she even answer if I called?*

I stop for a moment in the cold wind and stare at the highlighted name—Jenelle. My mind flips back to first grade.

We'd run around the playground at lunchtime, chasing each other in a game of tag with the boys. But in eighth grade, a group of girls who lived across the railroad tracks started bullying her. Jenelle was different from the other girls, wearing the same unicorn T-shirt for a whole year and taking a paper bag to school because her parents couldn't afford a backpack for her. It never bothered me though. She was a good friend. But those girls were brutal to her. *Who were those girls again?* I swallow. It wasn't that long ago but . . . I don't remember.

Everything changed when we started high school. After I got hooked on Fix, she turned away from me. I don't blame her. Lots of people did. But thinking about her now makes me miss her. She truly cared about me when we were little. Without hesitation, I call. What do I have to lose? Worst that can happen is she doesn't answer or doesn't remember me.

I let the phone ring once, then twice. *Maybe this was a bad idea.* Okay, a third time. *Mistake, hanging up now.* As I take the phone away from my face, I hear her voice.

"Hello? Penelope, is that you?" She must still have me in her phone.

"Yeah, it's me, how are you?"

"Good. Great! It's really good to hear from you!" The high-pitched tone of excitement in her voice is a relief to hear.

"So, you haven't forgotten about me then, huh?" I ask meekly.

"Penny, how could anyone forget about you?" No one's called me Penny since—well, since Tabatha passed away. I'll admit that feels good, too. "So, you busy?" she continues. "I get off work in a half an hour. I can pick you up. We could go somewhere and talk if you want."

Even though Jenelle and I haven't spoken in a long time, it seems she always knows what to say. I accept her warm invitation as I head into my backyard and make straight for the back door.

"Good! I'll give you a call when I'm ready," she says.

"Great, thanks."

"No problem. It was good to hear from you."

I thank her again and we both hang up.

The thought of meeting with Jenelle perks me up. I jiggle the ice-cold knob and pop the door open. A rush of warm air brushes my face. A steamy beef-flavored aroma lingers in the air. My mom must be making pot roast or something. The kitchen windows are fogged up and the stove dial is turned on. Maybe things aren't so bad after all.

"Mom? You home?" I yell out, taking my coat and shoes off by the back door. She doesn't answer. "Mom!"

I walk through the house toward the family room in the back to see if she's there. Sure enough, she is. And that scumball of a boyfriend of hers is, too. They're nearly having sex on the couch as Ken gropes under her shirt and she kisses the top of his head.

"MOM!" I scream out. Instantly they stop.

"Oh, honey, I didn't realize you were home."

"Yeah, well I wish I wasn't now," I groan, stomping back into the front room. "So, are you guys gonna be here long or what?"

"Shh, will you relax," my mom says, walking behind me until she catches up and faces me. "Listen, Penelope, I have a life, too. Don't act like I'm doing something wrong." She straightens her tousled, blonde mane of hair and adjusts her skin-tight outfit.

"Jesus, Mom, your boobs are still hangin' out. And that leather skirt? You shoulda got a size smaller, it looks too loose."

"Pen, stop being a smartass. What did I tell you about that?" She follows me into the kitchen and checks on the food.

"That for me?" I ask, pointing to the pot roast.

"It's for Ken and me." She closes the oven door and turns around to head to the table. "I didn't think you'd be here, to be honest." She grabs her purse and rummages through it. "Here, take this and get yourself something."

She holds out a twenty-dollar bill. I snatch it so she won't be able to change her mind.

"Thanks for buying me off, Ma."

"Look Penelope, I'll make you dinner tomorrow if that's what you want."

"I want you to be a normal mother. God, Sharon, just look at you."

"Don't call me Sharon. I'm your mother, for Christ's sake." She looks down at herself. "And besides, what's wrong with dressing like this? Ken likes it, so why do you care?"

"Of course Ken likes it. Don't you realize you look like a whore?" I point to her clothes again. "I mean, what mom dresses like that? Act your damn age!"

Before I can guard myself, she slaps me on the face.

"Go to your room, Penelope!"

"Screw you! I'm not five anymore!" I take my coat, slip my shoes back on, and head for the back door.

"Fine! Leave! God dammit, you're never around anymore anyway!" she screams out before I slam the door in her face.

CHAPTER NINE

The Burger Boy's line is long, crowded with hungry eaters. The scent of flame-broiled meat is making my stomach churn. But I order a cheeseburger anyway so I won't get hassled that I didn't buy anything. I take a seat in the corner by the windows, near the kid's zone area, to wait and watch for Jenelle. I called her on the way here. She should be coming any minute.

I take a tiny bite of my burger, pretending it's good, but it sucks. The meat is burnt and the cheese isn't melted. Man, and here I could be eating a good wholesome meal like pot roast, but instead my selfish mother and her leech of a boyfriend are hogging it all. She's such a bitch. She wasn't always this way.

When my dad and Tabatha were alive, my mom would always cook wonderful meals and we'd all sit around the kitchen table and talk about our day. My mom wasn't always worried about my dad's drinking back then. She'd say something to him like, "why don't you slow down," or "maybe that's enough," but that was it.

Even though my father drank heavily, it wasn't like he was a mean drunk or anything. In fact, he was jolly and happy, always laughing. It helped him to unwind. I don't think he would have drunk so much if he knew it would end his life so early. He was only forty-one when he passed away.

Tabatha took it harder than anyone. But I never thought she would jump off a high-rise building to deal with it. And I'm still not sure if that was her reason. She didn't leave me with a reason.

I found the suicide note in her top drawer, just days after it happened. I remember it word for word. *I hope that someday you'll be able to forgive me,* she wrote. *When the colors bleed a bright purple and pink, think of me. I'll be there for you, my Penny Girl.* I still don't understand why she did it. It just bothers me not knowing the reason.

I struggle to take another bite. *Screw it, I'm done.* I spit the bite out into a napkin and look out the window. Jenelle pulls up in a blue car in the front parking lot. She parks, gets out, and walks toward the side door. We go to different schools now, so it's been a while since I've seen her. But she looks as pretty as ever, with her rosy cheeks, so healthy in a pink glow. And her beautiful red hair—just as wild and long and full of curls as it always was.

She sees me and waves as she comes closer, taking a seat on the opposite side of the booth.

"Good, you're still here," she says with an amazingly white smile. I notice her braces are off. "I like what you did with your hair. The world needs more redheads, I always say." She situates herself, getting comfortable in the booth.

"Yeah, well it's not natural, like yours."

"Well, it looks good on you, something different. I like the haircut, too."

"Thanks." Goose bumps pop up along my arms, hearing all her compliments. I really don't know if it's just nervous talk, or if she really means it. She takes notice as I fidget in my seat a bit.

"So, tell me really. How are you?" She looks at me with her jade-colored eyes, like she's hoping to hear everything.

A few seconds pass as I look around to figure out how to begin, until she takes my hands, cupping them with hers and says again, "Pen, even though we haven't spoken since Tabatha's wake, I want you to know I am here for you always."

"I know." I yank my hands away and hold them close in my lap. "I know she loved me. She just didn't love herself enough."

"She was clinically depressed. It's not your fault." Jenelle's eyes are glossy. I'm not sure if it is because of the brisk wind from outside or if she's ready to cry.

"Come on," she says sweetly. "Let's talk about something else. So, what have you been up to?"

I want to tell her I'm still hooked on Fix and really struggling with quitting—that I've been going crazy seeing this imaginary guy. Rumors have been floating around school, but I think she may already know.

"Well, I haven't been doing much lately. Just hangin' out with Rose and that's about it."

Her face suddenly drops and turns an ashen gray.

"What? What is it?" I ask.

"You mean Rosario Rodriguez?"

"Yeah, why?"

"Remember when I was getting bullied a few years back?"

"Oh, don't tell me that was her?"

"Yeah, and her two friends. It bothers me to this day."

"I'm really sorry Jenelle. I didn't know."

"Yeah, well it's not your fault."

The whole mood between us changes for an awkward moment as silence infects our conversation.

Then Jenelle blurts out, "Have you heard about that one girl, Kelly Becker?" Changing the subject altogether.

"Yeah, it's horrible. Nobody knows what happened to her." I think she's just trying to switch to a new topic, but this is even more awkward than talking about Rose. I shrug it off and try to brighten up the conversation. "So, how are you? Anything new?"

She clears her throat and smiles, "Well, I'm finally dating again."

"Really, who?" My interest piques.

"Jared," she says. "You know, from grade school?"

"Jared-the-airhead Fletcher?" I ask.

She chuckles. "Yeah, but he's not really like that now. He's going to graduate early and is thinking of going into med school. Well, he does go to your school. Do you ever see him?"

"Sometimes, in the halls and stuff. Yeah, but wow, I would have never guessed it." I look out the window again, thinking of all the time that's gone by. I never meant for us to become so distant.

"So, you still with Walker?"

"Nah." I shrug my shoulders. "I moved on."

"Well, I don't believe that. Not at all. Not when he's been in love with you since, like what? The third grade?" Jenelle pauses for a bit. "I remember how much he drooled over you in class. And how you teased him about having another boyfriend, he'd get so mad. What did you call him? Man, it's on the tip of my tongue." She looks at me, waiting to hear the answer, but honestly, I don't remember. I have vague memories of my childhood. I think because I've been so drugged up.

Both of our minds wander off a bit. Jenelle looks around and over to the area where the kids are playing, maybe still trying to remember the name of this pretend boyfriend I teased Walker with. I really can't remember it. I look at the clock on the wall—6:47. All this reminiscing is great and all, but I think I should be going. I wonder if Rose is still having her party tonight. I don't want to be in a drug-induced circle, wiggin' out. I don't think that's going to help matters. But I don't want to go home tonight either. And then there's—

"Nate!" Jenelle blurts out. My face flushes and skips a beat.

"What did you say?" I ask as if I heard her say a foreign word.

"His name," she smiles, proud of herself for finally remembering. "That make-believe boyfriend you had. You called him Nate."

My heart nearly stops. I don't know what to say.

A wave of nausea swirls in my stomach. The bits of burger are rising in the core of my throat and are ready to lunge out. My upper lip sweats. This has to be just a weird coincidence . . . and yet. Did I know Nate before? Did I forget? I can't take this feeling. I need to make a run for it, and fast.

"Umm, Jenelle? Mind if I head to the bathroom real quick?" I ask, getting up and stepping backward.

"Sure, is everything okay, Pen? You don't look so good."

"Yeah, be right back."

I hurry into the women's restroom, push the swinging door open, and race into the first open stall I see. Crouching down, I vomit hard and spit remaining bits out afterwards.

"God," I say softly, curling around the toilet. "This is nuts!"

I take some toilet paper, wipe my mouth off, and flush. I stand up and brush myself off, making sure I haven't gotten any upchuck on me. Then I head over to a sink and wash my hands off.

My pocket buzzes. It's my phone. After I dry my hands with a paper towel, I reach for my phone and check to see whose calling. It's a text from Rose.

Where the hell are you? You said you'd be here! Get your ass over here, pronto! Oh, and call me asap. Let me know if you need a ride, too.

I text her back and tell her I will call her in a few minutes. I look at myself in the mirror. I'm as white as the bathroom walls and the feeling of puke lingers in my throat. But I take a few deep breaths, swing the door open, and go straight to the water fountains. As I bend my head down and slurp up a few cold sips, relief sets in.

I walk back over to Jenelle and tell her I need to go.

"Need a ride anywhere?" she asks, getting up to put her coat on.

"No, I'll be fine. I can have someone pick me up."

"Will you be okay?"

"Yes," I say sternly, trying to mentally prepare myself for this party. Do I really want to do this? It's possible others will be able to see Nate during the Fix circle. As far as I know, no one but me has seen him before.

Jenelle and I walk outside together to say our good-byes.

"Promise you'll call me?" Jenelle asks, shivering in the wind.

"Yeah, I promise. Thanks again, Jenelle." I wave good-bye as she heads over to her car.

I turn around and sneak off towards the west side of the building, trying to shake off what Jenelle just said. I can't understand it. How could I not remember something like that? Has the drug messed me up that much? I mean, I knew I would play and pretend a lot, but imagining Nate so long ago? It makes me wonder if it wasn't so pretend. Could Nate be more than just a figment of my imagination? More than a hallucination from the drug?

I call Rose. That's it. I'm taking Fix again. I need to get answers from the one who can really give them to me—Nate.

CHAPTER TEN

Clay arrives at 7:15. He's waving at me like a madman as he pulls into the parking lot. He's always been a goof that way.

When he's at the Burger Boy entrance, he rolls down the window and yells out, "Hey sexy thang, need a lift?"

"Will you stop messin' around!" I yell back. "So, did I miss anything?"

"No party is a real party unless you're there. Come on, get in." He signals for me to go around to the passenger side, so I corner the front of the truck. Clay revs the engine like he's going to run me over. I stop and wave my hands in the air and say, "What you waitin' for?" He laughs and waves me inside.

I hop in and put my seatbelt on. "So, what took you so long? I froze my ass off out there."

"Rose made me pick up some more beer first," he says as he pulls out of the lot and onto the street.

"So, how'd you get it this time?"

"Fake ID. Remember? I told you." He makes a sharp left, almost missing the green arrow. Beer bottles clank in the back and I tell him to be careful.

"So, who's there?"

"Oh, the usual." He looks at me for a split second and smiles. "And then some."

I wonder who it is this time. I know Rose's parents are

out of town, so Rose doesn't care how many people come to her house. Last time she had a party, the house got trashed and her parents had to spend a bundle on the cleanup. They didn't even care. Didn't punish her or anything. I guess that's what happens when you're an only child, and you're rich and spoiled.

"Man, there's some people I don't even know. You know how Rose is—the more the merrier. Ya know what I mean?"

"Yeah, I hear ya."

Clay turns down a few side streets and heads down Rose's block. We pull into the driveway and already the party's getting a bit out of control. There are people everywhere. Some on the porch. Some nearly on the neighbor's lawn. And a ton more inside. All the lights are on and the windows are wide open. Anyone passing by can see everything that's going on.

I unbuckle my seatbelt and am just about ready to get out, when Clay stops me. He grabs me by the wrist, startling me.

"Sure you're okay, Pen?" he asks, putting his hand on my thigh, making me feel a bit uncomfortable. "I'm always here for you, Pen, if you need me." He moves his hand off my leg and onto my shoulder.

"Clay!" I warn him.

"Yeah?"

"Umm, I think we should head inside now."

"Yeah, you're probably right."

I see Rose standing in the front window as we get out. She looks pissed, with her brows furrowed and her arms folded. I wonder if she saw anything. I don't want her thinking I'm making moves on her boyfriend—which I wasn't.

Clay was the one initiating things. I'm a little shaken by the whole thing. But I try to brush it off and pretend nothing's happened.

I climb the steps of the porch and peek through the front window, seeing if I recognize anyone. The usual crew is there, along with a few new faces. The crowd on the crammed porch is drinking and smoking and laughing it up. The night air is brisk and cold. But I guess when you get liquored up, you can be comfortable just about anywhere.

I look up at the clear, navy sky sprayed with flickering stars. The moon's nearly full, and lit up in a blue glow. When I walk inside, Rose greets me with a squeeze. I'm assuming she didn't see anything.

"Yo girl, you finally made it!" she says with a laugh. She takes her red Solo cup and heads into the kitchen.

The house is huge, with a big bay window in the front room and polished hardwood floors. The vibrant red couches look stylish against the mustard yellow walls.

Everyone's crowded around the monster-sized TV. Some are seated on the couch, drinking, while others play video games. It always amazes me how Rosario's parents keep things so clean even though they let her do anything she wants in the house.

I walk through the front room, trying not to step on the people lying on the floor. I tip-toe over the few guys sprawled out and make my way to the kitchen area, walking through the dining room first.

As always, Rose has a massive display of appetizers on the large mahogany table. Most of it is Mexican food, from tacos to guacamole and nachos galore. But she also pleases the picky eaters wanting more American-type food, from pizza bites to little hot dog roll-ups.

I take a Solo cup and head over to the fridge to see what there is to drink. A couple of girls are sitting at the small kitchen table. I try not to eavesdrop, but it's hard not to listen.

"Yeah, I can't believe she's really gone," the tiny brunette says.

"I know, it's been like a month already, and they haven't found anything," the girl with the blonde ponytail adds. "She's gotta be dead by now. She probably got all doped up on Fix and now her body's probably rotting in the woods somewhere or something. Aren't they always?"

"Don't say that! She was my friend! You didn't even know her!" a girl snacking in the dining room area turns around to say. "You have no clue what happened."

I try to remain invisible, pouring some Coke and putting the bottle back in the fridge. But for some reason, that doesn't work.

"Penelope, you remember her. What do you think happened to Kelly?" the girl in the dining room asks me. I recognize her from geometry class, but can't remember her name.

"Umm, seriously, I don't know. I really didn't know her very well." I take a small sip of the Coke and head downstairs where people are smoking heavily. The farther down I go, the more my lungs fill with cigarette smoke. As I step onto the backdoor landing, I stop and look outside, debating whether or not to go out to get fresh air. At that moment, a slender person, head covered with a dark hoodie, bumps into me. The person stops for a split second, then runs upstairs. Probably drunk.

I continue downstairs. The room is dimly lit and crowded, making it difficult to get to the basement.

Once I make it into the rec room area, I can't miss those unforgettable ice-blue eyes staring me down.

"What a surprise." Walker laughs, rolling his eyes. "Didn't expect you to be here." I hate it when he thinks he's so funny.

"Give it up, Walker," Clay cuts in, bending down to take a shot with the pool stick. "She ain't into you no more." Clay is always the first one to come to my defense. He has sisters of his own, so he's used to treating me like one of them. Then again, since that incident in the truck I really don't know how he feels about me anymore. Justin, who is standing on the other side of the pool table, laughs.

Off in the corner a big-boobed blonde is giggling. When I take a look, I see it's none other than Candace Roman. *Why would Rose invite her? And here I thought she hated her, too.*

I don't get too upset until she starts heading over to the black leather couch. She plops herself down next to Walker and giggles along with him. She hands him a beer, her annoying charm bracelet jingling. *I did not just see that. Just look away, Pen. Just look away.* But of course, I can't.

Walker and Candace huddle a little closer, whispering. He's got his arm draped across the cushion behind her. *Oh, please . . . how pathetic!*

"Surprised, huh?" Walker mumbles, looking at me again as I walk past them. Loud enough for me to hear, but low enough for me to blow him off. I am tired of his mind games.

For a split-second I wonder why I even bothered coming until Rose pops out of nowhere, grabbing my arm and dragging me to the bar. She shoots cold looks in Walker's direction and says, "Come on, let's get you a drink."

I take a seat on one of the black vinyl stools lined up against the thickly lacquered wood. Rose slinks behind the bar and starts mixing a drink.

"Man, Rose. Why Candace?" I whisper to her, watching her grab bottles from underneath the bar.

"Shh, listen, I can't stand her either. Believe me, I wasn't okay with it when Walker asked me." She grabs a stemmed wine glass hanging upside down from a rack above. "Here, you're gonna love this concoction. I just thought it up today." She pours vodka in the glass, along with lemonade, then a shot of rum, and a few drops of grenadine, making the drink turn pink. She slides the glass over to me and says, "Here, drink up. Let me know what you think of it, okay?"

I take a small sip and want to spit it out, but instead I swallow and let the burning mixture run down my throat. She looks at me wanting a response so I give her a smile and flip my thumb up.

I sit and continue to take small sips of my nasty drink, but am about ready to spit it back in the glass. My mind races around like a small kid with ADHD, not able to pay attention to one thing for too long. Clay and Justin are playing pool, while Walker and that skeeze make out. I'm not really bothered by it. Well, maybe a little. But deep down, I know it's all just a show because I'm here. In school, he acts like he couldn't care less about her. It seems Walker is more jealous of my "imaginary" Nate than I am of his newfound skank.

Rosario comes from around the bar and sits beside me. "Okay, so here's the plan," she says, pulling the stool up close to me. "We're gonna wait till it clears out a bit, since I only have a certain amount left to go around. The others aren't interested anyway. They were talkin' about going up to Hooter's or something and the rest are leaving around ten. So that leaves the six of us." Her eyes light up as she talks about the plan. Clearly, she's hooked on the drug. I just don't see myself that way. Then again, I haven't been very successful in quitting. Sometimes I wish Clay had never introduced us to Fix. If it wasn't for that damn party at the Tower, I wouldn't be in the position I am now.

Rose continues to explain the plan, getting jittery and excited as she goes on.

"Remember, if you close your eyes during the Fix circle, you have, like, no control," Rose says smiling. "Then again, that's the best part."

Everyone has a different experience on it. But when you join hands in the circle, anything goes. You can transport yourself to any place, be with anyone, and do anything. But you don't have control. Once you're in it, it's hard to get out. When the Fix wears off and you open your eyes, you're back to where you started—hopefully.

"So yeah, I am so jonesin' for it right now, it's not even funny," she whispers, cupping her hands up to my ear. "Don't tell Clay, but I snaked some from him. Just enough for the week."

"Rose, why?" I mumble. "He's gonna get so pissed off once he finds out."

"Oh, gimme a break, it was like only four or five pills. He won't even notice." She sniffles and wipes her nose. "Just don't tell Clay, all right?"

"Why would I?"

"Well, I'm just sayin'. Just don't." She looks at me like I'm a stranger. Or like she's confused. Her eyes are all glazed over and she keeps looking over her shoulder. I wonder if she's on it already. "So anyway, that's the plan. And you better be up for it, too."

One of these days I'm going to get the courage to tell Rose to stop bossing me around. But I don't think today's going to be that day.

CHAPTER ELEVEN

It's close to midnight and most of the people have cleared out. There's only a small group of guys lingering in the front room. Rose tries to coax them to leave.

She wanted me to wait for her in the kitchen, but I'm ready to go. The rest, including Walker and Candace, are downstairs and I'd rather not be there. But I'd rather not go home either. My mom doesn't care anyway, so why does it even matter?

"So, I'll see you guys tomorrow then?" Rose asks, twirling the tall guy's hair between her fingers. She's hanging all over him. Actually, all three of them. If Clay saw this, he'd kill her.

"Yeah, definitely. Thanks again, Rose," the shorter one with the buzz cut says. "I'll have it for you then."

I swear she's winning them over to get whatever she wants, which is probably more Fix.

She hugs and kisses them all on the cheek and waves good-bye. Rose walks over to me and smiles. "So, you ready?"

"I guess," I mumble, following her downstairs. "You know, I really don't think Candace should be in the circle. It could be dangerous for her. I just don't—"

"Don't worry about her," she says, cutting me off. "She's a big girl. She agreed, so that's that."

I give her a cautious, warning look—this isn't a good idea. For all we know Candace could have a bad reaction and die on the spot. There have been rare cases where that's happened. Either that, or you take too many and OD.

Heading downstairs, Rose blows me off. Instead of listening to me, she sort of rubs it in my face.

"So, Candace, you excited about gettin' Fixed up?" Rose twirls around to where Candace and Walker sit.

"You know you don't have to do this," Walker says, getting up to stretch. He seems hesitant about doing the Fix circle, too. Walker's usually against it. "I could take you home if you want."

Good! At least I'm not the only one who thinks Candace shouldn't be doing it. For once I agree with Walker.

"No way!" Candace jumps up to say. "Seriously, I wouldn't miss it for the world."

Oh, gimme a break! Walker already seems to like you enough to lip-lock you, why continue with this bullshit act? I swear, you're so fake. At this point I really don't care what she does.

"Good! What about you guys?" Rose looks over at Clay and Justin sitting by the bar.

"Hell yeah!" they say in unison.

"Do you need me to help you with anything?" Clay asks, sliding off the barstool. She nods and tells him something, pointing to the small closet in the corner.

"Okay, you guys, Clay's gonna get some chairs for us. Walker, can you make sure the back room's all cleared out?"

Walker checks out the room down the hall, while Rose directs Clay and Justin to move the chairs to the back room. That leaves me and Candace to stand around and wait.

"Did you want me to help with anything, Rose?" I ask

her—more or less beg her. Anything's better then standing around with big-boobs over here.

"Just make sure they don't break anything, okay?"

"Okay." I walk down the narrow hallway and head over to the back area. Candace follows. *Great!*

"I hope Rose won't ask me to move anything. I just got my nails done. See, don't they look nice?" Candace waves the gaudy fuchsia talons in my face as we walk.

"Candace, do you mind?" I motion for her to drop her hands. "What makes you think I even care?"

"Well, I know what you *do* care about." She gives me an odd smile, squinting her eyes. I take it she is referring to her hanging all over Walker.

When we get to the open doorway, the guys move a few things around. Walker and Justin prop the queen-size mattress up against the wall while Clay unfolds the chairs and forms a circle for six.

"Here, let's make some room," Rose says, pointing to the boxes in the center of the room. I walk over to help her, lifting a box, while Candace just stands there like a cheap plastic mannequin.

She asks us what to expect. Right then and there, my mind devises all the nasty things I could say to make her have a bad trip, like let the pill dissolve in your mouth and don't swallow it until all the liquid builds up. But if I did, she'd be puking her guts out on Rose's parents' plush white carpet. Who puts white carpet in their basement anyway?

"Well, if you want to get the best high in the circle, keep your eyes closed," Rose tells her. "It just gets really trippy if you open them during the circle. Unless you want that."

"Rose, don't give her any ideas," Walker interjects. "Just

stay in your seat and you'll be fine, Candace," he says, turning to her. She giggles and heads to the small bathroom across the way.

I still can't believe Rose is letting her in the circle. Rose hates her. There must be more to it than I know. The only thing I can think of is Fix. If there's a way for Rose to get more of it, then she'll do whatever it takes to make that happen. Even if that means befriending good ol' Candace Roman.

Rose and I stand by the doorway while Candace is in the bathroom, and the boys get more comfortable in the room. Everything's pretty straightened up now and the room actually looks nice. It's a spare bedroom that they never use, but it's fully decorated with oak paneling and the same plush white carpeting that's in the family room area. With the boxes in the corner and the mattress resting along the wall, the room itself is pretty big. The boys set up the chairs in the center of the room and everyone's now waiting for Candace to come out of the bathroom. *God only knows how long that will take.*

Rose sits on one of the chairs and reaches inside her pocket, pulling out a little plastic baggie with six black pearl-like pills. Just enough. She probably stashed the rest to make sure she has more for herself later.

"What the hell, Rose? You better not have smashed 'em." Clay lets out a worried sigh. After all, he's usually the one getting them from a dealer downtown, near the Tower. And I know how hard that can be. "They won't work if all the juice is squeezed out. God, how many times do I gotta tell you that?" While Clay's anxiety rises, Candace finally emerges from the bathroom.

"Chill out, they're fine. See, all fat and juicy," she says, standing up and holding the baggie up to his eyes. The pills roll back to the corner of the bag.

Walker and Candace each choose a chair and sit down next to each other. While Clay and Rose continue to argue about how she crammed them in her pocket, I look over the circle of chairs, not sure where I want to sit. I don't want to hold hands with Walker. And I certainly don't want to hold hands with Candace either. So instead of taking a seat, I wait, hoping to either sit next to Justin or Rose. After what happened with Clay in the truck, who knows where his hands might roam.

Candace steps over to Walker and gets all pissy when she realizes he isn't paying attention to her. She jerks his head to face her, and starts blasting off her complaint. *Ha! A girl telling Walker what to do? Let's see how long that lasts.* I watch their tiff for a moment, and notice how out of it he is. He's a little drunk, I can tell. Maybe he just doesn't care about what's going on right now. Maybe he's mad at me for earlier. I'm sick of analyzing him. If Walker has a problem with me, I wish he'd come out and say it. Until then, I'm kind of enjoying this. It's fun to see Candace bossing him around.

"Will you just sit down, Rosario," Clay demands, pointing to one of the empty chairs.

"Yes, sir!" Rose is always such a smartass when they fight. She takes a seat by Walker, with Clay following to her left. Justin takes it upon himself to sit by Candace, to her right, so that leaves one chair left. Even though that means I'll have to hold hands with Clay, I'd rather that than Walker or Candace.

Once everyone's situated, Rose lifts the bag of Fix above her head and shakes it. "You guys ready for this?"

Everyone is in agreement. Anxiety bubbles up in my brain as to how this is going to do down. I keep thinking about all the side effects Fix could have. I have a huge urge to bolt out of there—but Nate. I'm desperate to see Nate again.

Rose walks around the circle placing a pill into each open palm.

"Okay, everyone have one?" asks Rose.

Everyone either nods or says yes.

I stare at the pill in my hand. The black casing almost has a red tint to it in this dim light. I can't deny that it looks inviting.

"Okay, then. After you take your pill, make sure you hold hands with the people beside you. Now, on the count of three, everyone pop your pill, swallow, and then start holding hands. Ready? One . . . two . . . three . . ."

Everyone lifts a pill to their mouths and pops it in. We then hold hands. Justin's thin long hand is cold and clammy, while Clay's is warm, holding me with a firm grip.

As I close my eyes, I hear Candace giggling and Walker having a coughing jag.

"Shh . . . everyone be quiet," Rose whispers. "And keep your eyes closed."

Suddenly, everything gets so silent we can hear the crickets chirping on the other side of the cement walls, as if we started the circle outside. And when the temperature drops in the room, I begin to wonder if we *are* outside. But I try to focus on finding Nate. I hope he will appear during this high, but I'm not certain since it's in a circle. I've only done a few circles and Nate has never been there. I'm not sure why that is, if he's too uncomfortable materializing in front of a group or if he can't. I really don't know. And after what happened the last time I saw him, I'm not sure of anything anymore.

I try to focus on the blackness, hoping something will come into view. Nothing yet. Everything remains a waterfall of flowing black. At the same time, a wave of nausea comes on. My stomach feels as if someone's lifting it up from inside of me as the rest of my body remains bolted to the ground. The liquid that collects deep within my belly is starting to rise up my throat. Justin's hand to my left and Clay's hand to my right loosens and they let go.

Still nothing but waves of blackness, although I think I hear waves crash against rocks somewhere. I stand in the open air and hope I'm not near the edge of anything. It's cool and airy as I feel my way around. Nothing. I can taste salty ocean air, which stings my lips. Things finally come into focus. The darkness lightens into a midnight blue above me while the fog of misty sea air continues to roll in. I am completely by myself. Why?

"Rose? Walker? You guys here?" I urgently call out. The white carpet over the basement's cement floors softens into powdery sand between my bare toes. I feel naked, and when I look down I'm wearing a sheer white gown. The others, where are they?

"Hey, you guys? Can you hear me?" I yell out again, but no one responds. I don't understand why I am here and why I'm completely alone. I've never been alone during Fix circle. *What happened to everyone?*

I walk along the foaming white shore. Off in the distance I hear something. Faint whispers. Could that be them? I yell out again, "Walker? What the hell? Where are you guys?" But no one responds. I try to listen to the whispering but I can't make any of it out.

I walk through the sand, my feet sinking with each step, but I am making headway, passing trees along the shoreline. I get closer to the forest, stepping on rocks and weeds. I am careful not to step on anything sharp, but it's still hard to see. I'm not sure I want to go into the forest. At first everything's dark and I only see thick black leaves ahead of me. As I make my way through, there's a small orange glow far off into the distance. Thinking they've started a fire, I decide to head in that direction.

I spot a flash of yellow hair in the woods not too far from me. Sounds of leaves swish and rustle, like someone's running. A girl. When I get my eyes to focus, it looks a little like Candace. *Is that her?* It's got to be with that long yellow hair. She keeps looking behind her. There's light peeking through the trees and the faint whistle of an oncoming train. She runs out to the clearing and toward the railroad tracks off in the distance. That's when I see why she keeps looking behind her—someone's chasing her. It's a slender male, wearing a dark hooded jacket. I can't make out the face. He's too far away. Candace is trying to make it over the tracks before the train comes. Why is he chasing her? Who is he?

"Candace!" I yell out, but she doesn't hear me. In and out, she darts across the open field. Why is she so scared? "Candace!"

"Penelope . . ." A young man's voice emerges from behind, startling me. I turn around and stop in my tracks. "It's not safe," he whispers. It's Nate, but I can't figure out where he is.

"You must leave this place," he says.

I follow the sound of his voice into the thick, wooded area. It's nearly pitch black as I push the slick, leathery leaves back away from my face. It's impossible to see.

I rest my hand on a nearby tree trunk until I can catch my breath. My heart's beating so fast it feels as if it could stop at any moment.

I forge ahead and come to an area in the forest where it's even darker. Feeling my way through the blackness, I stumble across another large tree. Its huge trunk is brittle and hard and there's a warm, thick liquid running down between the grooves of the bark. As my hands trace down along the stream, the tree's bark starts to get soft and tender as the lines of the bark smooth out. I continue running my hands along the wet surface and realize it isn't just the tree I'm feeling, but flesh of some sort. *Oh my God! Someone's here!*

I step back in horror, unsure of what's there in the darkness. It isn't until the moonlight creeps out through the thick brush and shines pale blue rays across the tree that I see his face. And when his silver eyes flicker, I know.

"Penelope, it's not safe," Nate says. His weak body shivers as he tries to hold himself up and lean on the tree. "You must leave this place."

"What's wrong, Nate? What happened to you?" When he shifts his face in the light, I can tell he's been bleeding. The same dark liquid that was on the tree is running down his face.

"Don't trust your friends," he pants out, trying to calm down. "They know who I am."

"What are you talking about? Who knows what?" I beg him to answer but he's too weak. Slowly, his ailing body slumps down into the thick brush below.

"Nate! Get up! Please, what should I do?"

"You . . . you need to leave."

"No! Listen, I'm going to get help okay? Just hang on!"

I rest his head on a patch of soft moss, turning to run for help. I call out to the others as I go, but still no one answers. I'm unsure of everything. Who can I trust? Am I completely alone here?

After running in circles for what seems like an hour, I stop to catch my breath. And when I do, the glow I had seen earlier appears, brighter than before. I run toward it.

Voices emerge. I can't make out what they're saying. I peek through the leaves, inching myself closer for a better look. It's a group. They are hooded, in black clothes, dancing around a fire. Could it be a ritual of some sort? They don't look like the type to help, not by a long shot, so I curl back and stay hidden behind the bushes.

I decide to try for the coastline again. Maybe someone there could help? It's like walking in circles with thick foliage surrounding me. I try to focus on Nate and getting him help. I hope he's alright. And where the hell did Candace go? Why was she running? Who was that person chasing her? I don't understand. And I can't get over the fact that no one from the circle is here except for Candace and I only caught a glimpse of her. My mind is circling around so many questions and goes back to those masked people. I have a sick feeling it could be Rose and the others. As I make my way back to the beach, I second-guess myself. Maybe I don't know them at all. Maybe they're playing a sick prank on me. I just want out of this nightmare. I wonder why I am dressed like this, too. And barefoot no less. "Thanks a lot you guys, very funny," I say out loud. "Okay, the joke's on me, you can stop now!"

Nothing changes. And I can't stop my mind from getting ahead of me. *Pen, get it together. Think!*

As I make my way through the maze of foliage, I try to concentrate on the smell of the ocean air and the sound of the waves.

"Nate?" I whisper out into the nothingness. "If you can hear me, just hang on."

No sooner do I say that then I hear something rustling in the far-off bushes. My eyes scan between the dark leaves and branches and suddenly, from the corner of my eye, a shadowed figure moves.

"Nate, is that you?" I'm so scared at this point, I think my head is going to explode. This is becoming such a disastrous nightmare instead of a good high. I realize more than ever I am making the wrong decisions yet again. Why do I put myself through this crap?

"Nate, come on . . ." I call out again. "You there? Please let that be you."

"Yesss . . ." A voice slithers out through the trees. "Your Nate is near, come, Penelope."

This time, I can't tell who the hell's voice it is. It's muffled; it's too hard to tell.

"Don't go in there, Penelope," another voice says off into the distance. I'm so confused by all the voices. I don't know who to listen to. I become so suspicious I freeze in my tracks, not knowing what to do or where to run.

Then everything stops.

Nothing. I hear nothing. Just dead silence. Huge dark clouds gather above me, blanketing the silver moon. Suddenly, straight in front of me, two black-clothed figures pop out from behind the bushes.

"Come and see," one of the muffled voices say. The other grabs my arm and drags me through the forest. "It is time."

"Time for what? Where are you taking me?" I scream, trying to pry their hands off me. "Who are you?"

One of the dark figures turns around, looking at me

through the small slits in the cloth covering its face. "It's time for you to know. You must come now and see."

"Let me go," I demand, but its grip is so tight, the circulation in my arm is getting cut off. They're taking me back to their camp. The glowing light is getting closer and closer. Twigs break around my body as they drag me until finally we make it to the clearing. There are a few other masked figures standing near the fiery glow, chanting, "Burn him, burn him."

When they let me go, I drop to the ground. I look up in horror. Oh my God, no! They have Nate tied to a wooden cross. They're going to torch him!

"Please, stop! He's done nothing to you!" I cry out, trying to get to my feet. Nate struggles to pry himself loose. I slowly back away.

Suddenly, someone grabs me from behind. I scream out, "Let me go!" But when I turn around and see the flash of blue eyes, I know who it is.

"Shh . . . be quiet," Walker says, covering my mouth with his hand as he pulls me into the brush and wrestles me to the ground. "Something went terribly wrong. We need to get out of here."

"But how?"

"Do you trust me?" he asks, holding me close, smothering me with his body. I can feel the rush of terror in his voice. Nate's message, *don't trust your friends*, surfaces in my mind. But it's Walker. "Penelope, do you trust me?"

"Yes . . . why? What's going on?"

"I don't know. One minute I'm on the beach with Candace and the others and the next, she's gone. They're all gone."

His breathing is heavy as he looks around to see if we've been spotted.

"What do we do?"

"There's only one thing I can think of," he whispers. "We need to escape."

"But how? We can't just leave the others."

"Do you wanna stay here? It's our only shot at getting the hell outta' here."

"I can't. I can't leave Nate."

"Penelope! He isn't even real! You've got to listen. We need to leave."

He looks around again, eyeing up the masked figures surrounding Nate. When I look back, Nate's ready to slip out of the ropes. He mouths, "Run." I want so badly to help him, but I'm at a loss. The only way out is to stick with Walker.

"We'll have to make a run for it," he says. "Here, take my hand."

We get up, holding hands tight. Walker orders, "Now!" and we dart through the forest. He squeezes my hand tighter and tighter, telling me not to let go. My heart's beating faster than I think is possible. I have the urge to look back, but I'm too scared.

"Hurry." Walker commands. "There, to the rocks."

"But the edge?"

"Just do it."

Faster and faster we run, until we get to the edge. Thankfully, they haven't followed us. I can only hope Nate made it out of there. Walker takes my other hand and holds it tight as he looks me in the eye.

"We need to jump."

"What? Are you crazy?"

"It's the only way to force us to go somewhere else."

Walker wraps his arms around my waist and holds me close with a firm embrace.

"Ready?"

We both look outward, ignoring the ragged rocks hundreds of feet down below us. I think about Tabatha, jumping to her death. I shudder.

"Ready."

Hugging each other close, we both take a few steps out until we drop into thin air, like a roller coaster heading straight down. Then an unknown force drags us deep into the nothingness and everything turns black.

CHAPTER THIRTEEN

I wake up on the floor somewhere. It's the same plush carpeting at Rose's house, but I'm still not sure where I am. Then, from the faint sounds of crickets chirping, I know I'm safe. Everything's dark and quiet. Feeling my way around, I grab onto a chair, get up, and slowly make my way toward the wall and the light switch. When I flick the light on, I see Walker lying on the floor off in the corner.

"Wake up," I tell him, running to him, shaking him back and forth.

"Huh?" He wrestles around a bit, opening his eyes. "Where are we?"

"We're back at Rose's place."

He sits up and rubs his eyes. "So where is everyone?"

I look down the hallway and back at him and tell him I don't know. Both of us move slowly, trying to recall what happened. We're back in the same room we started from. That's for sure. Nothing seems to have changed except for no one being here but me and Walker.

"Come on, let me help you up." I take Walker's arm and help bring him to his feet, and sit him down on one of the chairs. "You gonna be all right?"

"Yeah, yeah." He waves me off, holding his head. "Go look for the others. I'll stay right here."

I walk out into the hallway and to the rec room, but no

one's around. I turn on a few light switches in case I missed something, like someone passed out on the couch or behind the bar for some reason, but nothing.

I head to the stairs, walking up to the landing where the back door is and look outside. Clay's truck is parked outside the garage, so maybe they're all out there. But instead of running outside, I check upstairs first.

The place is trashed. There are cups and plates of food everywhere and the lights are on, so I'm thinking someone's got to be here besides me and Walker. Where else could they be?

"Rose? Clay? You guys here?"

I check the clock on the wall, 5:25 in the morning. The faint sounds of the TV are coming from the front room. The eerie flicker lights up the dim room. It's turned to a news channel. What catches my attention is that they're talking about Fix. I grab the remote and turn up the volume.

"Reports say that Fix, although illegal here in the United States, is becoming increasingly common with teenagers today. More and more deaths are being linked to the drug," the dark-haired newscaster says. "Studies show that children as young as twelve years old are susceptible to addiction."

I am spooked, and feel a chill run down my spine. I quickly turn off the TV. I check in the side bedrooms and the bathroom really quick. Nothing. Once I turn back into the front room area, I head to the upper floor. Maybe Rose went to sleep?

I get to the upstairs landing and go into what I think may be Rose's room, as I've never been up here before. After turning on the light, I'm surprised at what I see. It certainly isn't something I would expect of Rose. It's purple, with lace curtains and knickknacks of unicorns and horses. My eyes catch sight of trophies on the other side of the room. Rose talked about gymnastics sometimes, but she never told me how good she was.

I look around the room. On her dresser, there's a picture that catches my attention. It's of her with her gymnastic teammates. I lift the picture to get a closer look. I went to grade school with a lot of the girls in the picture. When I spot Rose, I can't believe who's sitting right next to her. Could that be? No way.

I squint my eyes and examine the picture closely. And from those big bright eyes and that long yellow hair, it's got to be Candace. *God, Rose, you were friends with her when you were little?*

I keep staring at the picture with trembling hands and notice another familiar face. Kelly Becker. I glance at the other pictures propped on her dresser. There's one with the three of them huddled together in their gymnastic outfits.

All three of them used to be friends.

I set the picture down, hearing muffled voices outside in the backyard. Looking out the window, I see Rose, Clay, and Walker standing by the garage, talking.

I race downstairs, to the kitchen door in the back. Swinging the door open, I go straight to where they're standing. Walker's already having words with them.

"Why'd you do it?" Walker demands, raising his hands up. "And where the hell did Candace go?"

"I don't know what you're talking about. Why'd we do what?" Rose lashes back at him. "And what the hell happened to you guys anyway? I mean, both of you just flaked out on us. We tried waking you guys up. But both of you were in such a deep sleep, we couldn't."

Clay looks like he wants to say something but doesn't.

"Are you sure it was Fix that you gave us and not something else?" I ask.

"Positive," Rose says. "You think I would do that to you guys?" She turns her back and holds her hands up to her face. I wouldn't put it past her. I want to say something, but I keep quiet and let them explain.

Clay pipes up. "Look, after we woke up, Candace complained. She said she needed to get home since it was so late. Justin walked her back. And you two, well, like Rose said . . . you two were still passed out cold. What were we supposed to do?" Clay tells us. "I just talked to Justin a little bit ago. Candace made it home fine."

"I don't know," Walker says in a worried voice. "Something doesn't sound right. I just don't get how me and Penelope didn't wake up when we were supposed to. Can either of you tell me just what the hell happened in that circle?"

"Yeah, why weren't you guys in the high? Where was everyone?" I demand, but Clay and Rose have nothing to say. For a long few minutes, everyone stands in silence. "Hello? What the hell, did you not hear me? What happened?" I wave my hands in Rose's face, ready to slap the skin off her.

"Listen," Clay tells me, backing me up off Rose. "Seems like everyone had a different experience. You guys weren't in mine and Rose doesn't remember you guys being in hers either. And from what Justin and Candace said, they had a pretty bad high, too. No one was in anyone's."

"That's not true. Walker and I were in the same high.

And I could have sworn I saw Candace, too. Why was that, then?" I ask.

"Yeah, she's right. Both of us were together. You guys were there in the beginning but disappeared shortly after," Walker pipes in. "So, tell us, how can that be?"

Rose groans. "God, don't you guys get it? It's a mind-altering drug. Sure, there's going to be some kind of connection with someone else in the circle, but no one is going to experience the same thing. You share dreams with people you have the most connection to, or whoever's on your mind most. Just because we're all in the circle together, doesn't always mean we're in the high together, too."

"Fine, whatever. It's still messed up to me," I tell them. "It just seems like someone's not telling the whole truth."

"Pen, calm down. You're fine now, aren't you?" Clay asks.

Yeah, I think. *I'm fine, but what about Nate?* I can only imagine their laughter if I share my concerns about him.

"Whatever, it's late." I look at my phone and see that it's after six already. "I've had enough of this shit. Later, people."

As I am heading down the driveway, Walker stops me.

"Are you going to be okay walking home?"

"Yeah, I think so," I tell him. "It's only about a twenty-minute walk from here."

"Will you be in school later? I don't want to have to worry about you."

"Don't. I'll probably go for third period. Just to get some more sleep. But I'll be there."

I turn around and walk down the winding sidewalk to the end of the block. When I get to the main street, I decide to walk under the streetlamps lining the road. Normally, I would cut down side streets and head into the darker part of the neighborhood, but I don't want to get jumped by some freak. Not after all the crap that's just happened. Not for anything.

As I walk, the scent of raw melting metal mixes in the early morning air, engulfing me with thoughts of Nate. I lick my lips and it tastes like blood. I look around and see no one, yet I get an overwhelming sense he's here with me. Or maybe that's just wishful thinking, I don't know.

I keep walking and check my phone to see if I have any messages. There's a few from my mom, so I press to listen to my voice mail.

"Where are you, Penelope? It's eleven-thirty. Please call me. Please. I'm sorry about earlier. Just call me," her voice pleads. She left two more similar messages. I know my mom and I don't get along very well, but I still love her and feel bad that she's been worrying about me. I get to the end of Bellwood Street and turn the corner, picking up speed as I head toward home.

All the lights are on in the house. I can see my mom pacing back and forth through the front windows. She keeps checking her phone every other second.

I really didn't mean to fight with her earlier. It's just that I can't stand it when she acts like that. After my father passed away, what made her want to turn into a slut like that? Is she that lonely? I know she had it even harder when Tabatha died, but still. It's not like I turned into a slut, too. But I did turn to drugs so I'm not really any better.

I go walk up the driveway and into the yard toward the back door.

"Mom, I'm home!" I yell out.

Running into the kitchen she cries out, "Thank God, you're back. I was just about ready to call the cops."

She hugs me tight and tells me how much she loves me and how sorry she is about the fight we had earlier in the day. I stand there letting her hold me for a while. I have to admit, it doesn't feel all that bad. I want us to be close again but I don't know how to approach her anymore. We should be closer than ever after what happened to our family and all, but instead we've grown further and further apart.

"So, the punk is finally home, I see." Ken slithers out, walking into the kitchen. "Good. Maybe now you should put a leash on her, Sharon."

"He's still here?" I pull away, looking at her with hatred and disappointment. "What the hell's the matter with you, Mom? Don't you see what a prick Ken is?"

"Listen, Penelope, he's been here to help me," she says, following me into the front room as I start up the stairs. "Please, will you just listen? I need someone, too."

"I understand that," I say, stopping midway up the stairs. "But why does it have to be a jerk like him?"

"Fuck you, you little shit! Why don't you go back out and disappear!" Ken spits out.

"See, Mom!" I run up the rest of the stairs and turn around on the landing. "Are you even hearing any of this?"

She follows me as I head to my room.

"Will you just give him a chance? It doesn't have to be this way."

"You know what? Just forget it. It's a lost cause." I swing the door closed in her face, lock it, and plop down on the bed. I could cry right now. But I haven't the tears. I can only hope I can get this crappy day out of my mind and pray tomorrow will be better.

CHAPTER FOURTEEN

I wake up with a splitting headache. Stomach cramps invade my insides and won't stop. I don't think I'm getting my period, so that's not it. Plus, my nose is all crusty for some reason.

When I lift my head off the pillow I notice dark, bloody stains. *Was my nose bleeding again?* Once I get out of bed, I take the pillowcase off, throw it in the hamper, and go straight to the bathroom to check.

There's a long streak of crusted blood running down the side of my cheek and into my hair. I grab a washcloth off the towel bar, turn the water on, and scrub my face. *Man, it's on my shirt, too.*

I glance outside the bathroom toward my nightstand where the digital clock is. The red glowing numbers read 10:43. *Damn! I'm late.* Normally, I would just ditch, but I promised Walker I would be there when third period starts at eleven, so I hurry to get ready.

After putting on some fresh clothes and brushing my teeth and hair, I grab my phone and some money from my dresser and head out.

I walk as fast as I can in the brisk morning air. The temperature has got to be around freezing because the ground is covered in a light frost and my breath plumes out. If I had Tabatha's car, I wouldn't be so late. With the couple of dollars in my pocket, I make a mental note to take the Red Line to the Tower after school. If Clay doesn't want to take me, I'll go myself. I'm not even sure if I want Clay to take me anyway. I really don't know what he, Rose, and Justin are up to, but I'm seriously thinking hanging around them isn't a good idea anymore. Just seems like one big headache—literally. *Don't trust your friends.* I hear Nate's words in my mind.

The cramping in my stomach has subsided. Maybe the walking has helped. Either that or breathing the cold air, I don't know.

Thoughts of last night swim inside my head like hungry sharks looking for their next meal. Who were those hooded people? What did they want with Nate? Is Nate okay?

I have the urge to take Fix again, and not just to find out if Nate's okay, but I want desperately to escape from this mental anguish. And the more I take Fix, the more stuff happens that I can't seem to correct.

After I cross 100th Street, I face the entrance of the school. Inside, the receptionist in the front office calls me over, asks for my ID card, and gives me a yellow tardy slip. It takes her a few minutes before she returns the ID to me as she continues to look at the computer screen. *I hope she doesn't say anything about all the times I ditched lately.*

"Is there something wrong?" I ask, tapping my fingers on the counter. My heart speeds up while my mind conjures some lie in case she asks about my absenteeism.

"Hold on, I need to put something into the computer. It will just take a second."

She types something into the computer and gives my ID card back to me.

The end of the second period bell rings and everyone

files into the halls. The smell of books and the different colognes people are wearing make me sick. A wave of nausea seeps through my system like a dark force taking my body over. I head to the girl's bathroom, ready to throw up.

Swinging the door open, a few girls are already swarming the mirrors. It never fails. And not just any girls—Candace's clones, Emma and Brandy. But I don't see Candace.

I enter the nearest stall and slide the lock across the closed door. I'm glad they don't notice me.

Gathering my bearings, I hover my head over the toilet and take a few deep breaths. Even though the bathroom smells nasty, I begin to feel better. I try to hold the upchuck back, thinking it would be totally embarrassing to vomit with them in here.

"Yeah, I can't believe it either," Brandy says. "Her mom called me, too, last night. She told me she had to file a missing persons report this morning."

"Well, the last time I talked to Candace was when she was getting ready to go to that chick's house. What was her name?" Emma asks.

My stomach drops.

"That Rodriguez girl from Spanish class. Remember she told you?"

"Oh, that's right."

What the hell! Candace didn't make it home last night? What happened to her? I wait a few minutes for Brandy and Emma to leave the bathroom before I emerge from the stall. But as the bathroom door bangs shut, I swing right back around into the stall. All the things that were fighting to stay in my stomach come out. I hurl up hunks of the appetizers

I had last night at Rose's. Little hot dog bits and chunks of pizza all come spilling out and into the toilet.

After I vomit, my stomach settles. Things seem better. Then again, how good can things be when Candace is missing, too? What if I get questioned by the police? They will find out I'm using Fix. My nerves bundle up tighter and tighter.

Why are Rose and Clay lying? Did Justin really walk her home? Did he have something to do with this? I have the urge to talk to him to find out his version of the story. Will he even tell me what happened?

Everyone crowds into the room for seventh period health. It's the only class I have with Justin. After I take my seat in the last row to the right, Justin walks in and sits a few rows ahead of me. Before class starts I motion to him, waving my hand and calling his name.

"Psst, Justin, over here."

He turns around to look my way.

"I need to talk to you after class. Will you wait for me?"

"Yeah . . . sure," he says, turning back around in his seat.

The rest of the students take their seats as Mrs. Devons prepares for class to start. She shifts around papers on her desk, takes a marker, and writes something on the whiteboard. After she moves away, the words "FIX ME" pop out in bold letters.

"Can anyone tell me what that means?" Mrs. Devons asks, looking for any takers from the rows of students, but no one raises their hands. "Anyone?" she asks again.

Davey Munns, the class clown, raises his hand in the air and she points to him to answer. "It means you want to be fixed?" he says with a snickering laugh. The whole class murmurs and mumbles and laughs along with him.

"In a way, yes. Can anyone tell me anything else?"

"It means you want to get high on Fix," Tina Waxman, with her perfect hair and her perfect clothes, blurts out. Obviously, that's what the teacher's driving at. Tina, the perfect girl and teacher's pet, would have to state the obvious.

"Yes, that's right Tina. Today we are going to talk about Phixeedifore, also commonly known as Fix." The teacher picks up a box behind her desk, rummaging through it and starts passing out blue pamphlets to the class. As the pamphlets distribute up and down the rows, there's a knock at the door. It's one of the ladies from the attendance office. After Mrs. Devons invites her in, they huddle off to the side and talk. They both keep looking my way. I wonder if it's because of what the front desk receptionist wrote in the computer earlier.

"Miss Wryter, Mrs. Evans would like to have a word with you," Mrs. Devons says, pointing for me to leave the room. "Please take your things and go to the counselor's office immediately."

Man, I knew it! She did put something about me in the computer.

I get up and leave the room, walking down the east wing of the school to the attendance office. Girls from the decoration committee are setting up tables and blowing up balloons to sell tickets for the Blast from the Past dance. There's a tall kid with blonde, shaggy hair buying tickets. It isn't until he turns around that I notice it's Jared, Jenelle's boyfriend.

"Oh, hey, Penelope!" Jared stops me as I head to the

main office. "Good timing. I've been meaning to talk to you. You have a sec?"

"Sure, what's up?"

"Well, Jenelle's been telling me a lot about you lately. Is everything okay?"

Like I'm going to tell him all my problems. I nod my head. "Yeah, everything's fine."

"Listen, I'm buying a block of tickets for the dance. Jenelle's been begging me to go. I thought maybe you and some of your friends would want to come?" He tries to hand me some tickets.

"Well, I don't know. I'm not really into that kind of thing."

"Here," he urges again, putting them in my hand. "I think Jenelle would love to see you guys there. She's always talking about you. You can decide later."

"Well, I guess. Umm, I'll think about it."

I thank him, take the tickets, and turn around, heading back down the hall.

In the main office, a gray-haired attendance lady tells me to have a seat and wait. It isn't long until Mrs. Evans comes in to get me. She must be younger than my mom with her long, brunette hair pulled back in a ponytail and her slender, athletic body.

"Miss Wryter, I'm ready for you now. Come with me," Mrs. Evans says, motioning to her office down the narrow hallway. "I'm glad to see you made it."

I enter her office, and she tells me to take a seat as she sits down behind her desk.

"So how are you, Miss Wryter?"

"It's Pen. Just Pen."

"Fine, Pen. So, tell me. How are things at home?"

"Okay, I guess."

"And your friends? Getting along with everyone?" She smiles, pulling her seat closer to the desk.

"Uh huh." I wiggle around in the chair, trying to keep my jittery legs still, but it really doesn't help. I just wish she'd get to the point already.

"Good, that's settled. I wanted to talk to you about the e-mails I've been getting from your teachers. They say you've been skipping class. Can you tell me why that is?"

"I don't know," I mumble.

"Well, Penelope, if this keeps up, you'll have a hard time graduating." She's right. And I want to graduate. Really, I do, but this struggle with Fix has me so tangled.

"I'm sorry, Mrs. Evans. I really didn't realize how bad it was."

"Listen, I know it's been rough for you, but I think you can do better."

"You're not going to call my mom about this, are you?"

"Not if I see an improvement. Right now, this is just a warning."

"Thank you, Mrs. Evans. I'll do better."

After she nods her head and excuses me, I get up and walk out of the office in relief. I'm glad she wasn't too strict. I know I shouldn't be ditching class so much. And yes, graduation is on my mind. I know how hard it is to find a job without a high school diploma.

I head back to seventh period as the bell rings and fight the current of kids spilling out into the halls. Back in the room, I notice Justin's already gone. *Damn him!* So much for waiting.

Last period ends and class lets out. I want so badly to talk to Nate—about everything. I hope he's okay. I need to get Fix from somewhere. I really don't want to get high with Rose and her friends, so I'm hoping to go to the Tower later on. I'll take the 95th Street bus down to the Red Line and walk to the Tower. I'm really hoping to connect with Al and find Tabatha's car, too.

I make one quick stop at my locker and grab a little more money for the trip. I've stashed a few twenties in a small brown bag on the top shelf. Forty bucks should be enough.

I slip the money in my back pocket, and slam the locker door shut. From the corner of my eye, I see through the window Rose, Clay, and Justin milling around outside. I figure now's the best time to talk to Rose. I don't want to have to confront her, but I need to know more about last night. I'm not sure who's been questioned by the police, but I'm sure they're going to make their rounds. I'm worried about what happened to Candace. Even though I can't stand her, I wouldn't want anything bad to happen to her.

I take a deep breath to keep my nerves together as if they were a ball of yarn. But I feel they can unravel at any moment. I don't want to fall apart when I talk to Rose. Sickness settles in the pit of my stomach, and is slowly traveling upward. I've got to keep it down. Wouldn't want to throw up on anyone. That would be totally embarrassing.

I walk through the wave of kids cluttering the halls. It's the same thing every day. No one seems to ever pay attention—especially the ones texting and not watching where they're going.

I glide and make my way through the maze of people, getting to the side entrance. A cold gust of wind travels underneath my coat, sending chills down my spine.

At a fast pace, I head straight to the corner. None of them see me yet. It's too crowded. As kids start clearing out, it becomes easier to walk. Justin, Clay, and Rose are huddled together with their backs turned toward me. It isn't until Clay and Justin turn around that Clay tugs Rose's arm to let her know I'm coming.

"Oh, hey you!" Rose yells out, opening her arms as if wanting a hug. "We're just going to White Castle to grab a bite to eat. Come with us."

I stare at her for a minute. She's acting like nothing's happened. I want to scream in her face, "What the fuck is the matter with you?" but I hold back. Now is not the time to jump down her throat, so I agree to go with them. When the light turns green, we cross the street together and make our way to White Castle.

Clay opens the door for everyone and we enter.

"Let's sit over there," Rose says, pointing to the empty booth in the corner. "Clay, order us some sliders and a few drinks."

He nods and walks with Justin to the counter, while Rose and I sit down. She seems more jittery than ever, bouncing her legs underneath the table and strumming her fingers.

She keeps looking over at Clay and Justin, and Justin keeps looking back at her. I wonder why he keeps looking at me and Rose, like he's worried about something.

I turn to her and decide to stop beating around the bush.

"Rose, what the hell happened last night? What happened to Candace? Tell me the truth, Rose."

"I'm not sure what you're talking about, nothing happened. And I'm not sure what happened to Candace either. I told you what I know." She looks down and at her watch, like she's got somewhere to go, and again at Justin and Clay. "What the hell's taking so long?"

"Don't you even care what happened to Candace? Aren't you worried about the cops? What the fuck happened in the circle, Rose?"

"Everything's going to be fine. Candace will turn up, I'm sure."

"How do you know that? You're acting like you don't even care? First Kelly Becker, and now another missing girl! And we were the last ones to see her. Where's your compassion?"

"Look, all I know is that Justin walked her home." Again, she looks at Justin as he looks back at us from the checkout line. "Or some of the way home or whatever."

"Oh, so it's *some* of the way home now?"

"Justin wouldn't lie to me, Pen. He mentioned something about her not wanting to get caught with a guy that late at night. So, he didn't walk her all the way home but he made sure she was okay. I wouldn't worry about it."

It sounds like she's trying to convince herself it was not her fault. My anger continues to mount.

"Rose! Don't you get it? Candace is gone!"

Just as I'm about to say more, the boys walk up to the

table. Clay and Justin stand there with a tray of cheese-burgers and two large Cokes, looking at us. Rose motions for them to sit down. It's like they have to ask her first for everything. I don't get it. Clay sets the tray down as Justin asks us what we're talking about.

"Don't worry about it, Justin," Rose snaps at him. "Just eat your food and be quiet."

"Is this still about last night?" Clay asks before chomping down on a burger. The smell of the warm, greasy, fried crap is making my stomach churn. I'm ready to throw up again. "Pen? You okay? You don't look so good."

"No, I'm not okay." I get up and run to the bathroom, bang the stall door open, and start dry heaving. Not much is coming out but juicy spit. I stand there for a bit, taking in deep breaths, then head to the sinks. Pressing the knob and letting the water fall, I take a few long sips. After, I blot wet paper towels on my face.

"What is she hiding?" I whisper softly into the bathroom mirror. I don't know, but my gut is telling me Rose knows a lot more than she's saying. Her story keeps changing.

I get myself together, straighten up, and head back to the table. Already they're cleaning up and getting ready to leave.

"Justin!" I call out. "Did you really walk Candace home?"

A stunned expression crosses his face. He opens his mouth as if to speak, but nothing comes out. Like he doesn't know what to say. Justin looks at Rose as if needing per-mission to speak.

"Justin! What the hell? Don't you know?" I ask again.

"I just told you, Pen. Why do you keep asking?" Rose interjects. "Listen, we're leaving. Just drop it." She gets up and slides out of the booth. "You're welcome to come by later to get high with us. But seriously, don't keep asking me about last night. It's over, ya got it?" She looks at me with dagger eyes ready to pierce into me. I take that as a threat. I don't want to fight her or get on her bad side. I've seen her fight, and have seen the other girls after. I wouldn't want to be that other girl. In some small way, I can understand how Jenelle felt when she was bullied by Rose. So, I nod my head and agree to not bring it up again. There's got to be another way to figure out what went down during the circle last night. I am determined to find out.

I keep my distance as they start to leave.

Rose waits by the door as Clay throws the trash away. Justin stands there looking like a third wheel until Rose calls him over. Why does she have such a hold on them? I mean, they totally act like her puppets. Seriously brainless.

I wait for them to leave, watching them cross the street and walk down the block before I decide to head outside. Once they're gone and out of sight, I walk to the bus stop and wait under the shelter.

The sky is overcast as a cold and dreary rain threatens. *Great! All I need is to get stuck in this crap.*

Watching the cars zoom by, I pop my head out of the shelter to watch for the bus. I have nothing better to do than think. I take a seat on the bench and wonder how it got to be this way.

I glance over to the school and think about when I first started at Mayford High. Freshman year was an eventful one to say the least. All my classes were screwed up and I had a horrible schedule. The first class of the day was gym and I couldn't stand it because I got sweaty first thing each day. But that's where I met Rose.

I was sitting on the bleachers in the gymnasium, all the way at the top—minding my own business. Some of the girls like Candace and her clones were laughing and joking around. Apparently about me, I guess, because I was sitting alone. They figured I was easy to pick on. But Rose put an end to that quickly after she made a smart remark about Candace's makeup. It was funny to see Candace nearly cry in embarrassment.

Rose decided to sit with me throughout the whole period. She was a real jokester and smartass. No one could mess with her.

I look up across the street and spot a slender male dressed in black with his hood up, staring straight at me. My heart nearly stops. I can't make out his face. It's blurry for some reason. I rub my eyes, thinking maybe it's another side effect of Fix.

Nate. "Is that you?" I say under my breath. I keep staring at him, hoping my eyes will focus. I want to run across the street and hug him, but the traffic is too busy.

I stand up and walk to the curb for a closer look and his eyes flash silver in the sunlight and my heart jumps.

"Nate!" I scream out, cupping my hands to my mouth. I dance back and forth and wave feverishly. I must look like a madwoman.

Cars and trucks zoom by, and I step on a rock and look down. When I look back across the street, he's gone.

Twenty minutes later, the bus still hasn't come. I don't know if that was Nate or not. Maybe it was someone else. *God, I'm not even high.* It couldn't have been him.

I zip my parka up higher as the wind continues to blow, still feeling jittery over what just happened. Confusion twists my thoughts into one huge knot, making my head pulse. I need to get to the Tower to get Fix and find out for sure what happened to Nate. Finally, the bus comes. I step on and slide my money into the pay machine. The doors close behind me and the bus jerks into motion. I walk down the narrow aisle and take a seat in the back row.

I know this is probably a bad idea to go to the Tower again, but it must be done. I need to know for sure if Nate's okay. *God, and Tabatha's car.* I almost forgot.

CHAPTER SIXTEEN

I get off the Red Line on Harrison Street. It's getting dark and cold. I wish I wore a warmer coat.

I see the Tower in the distance as I walk. Looming over the rooftop is that same dark cloud. It's so strange, too. I usually only see the cloud when I'm on Fix.

I turn the corner and dart across the street to Al's Parking Lot. An old Hispanic guy in a gray jumpsuit is working the booth. I run past the graveled lot, march up to him, and explain my situation.

"Excuse me, sir, I'm looking for my car. Can you help me?"

He's looking at me like I'm some strange animal he's never seen. I'm not sure he understands me.

"It's a white Oldsmobile Cutlass. I parked it over there." I point to the spot I last parked it.

He just shakes his head. He doesn't seem to understand English. I'm getting nowhere with this. Frustrated, I decide to go to the trailer across the lot, hoping I will see Al and find out more.

I cross the parking lot, walk up the trailer's ramp, and knock on the door. Lights are on inside, but no one is answering. I knock again. I take a look around. There aren't many cars in the lot. Business must be slow tonight. I peek into the small window next to the door and see if anyone's inside. The place is a pigsty with boxes everywhere and trash all over the place. I can barely see Al's desk off in the corner.

I walk to the other end of the trailer to see if there's another door. I look into the side parking lot that's all gated up. From the corner of my eye, peeking out between two cars, I see it. *It's right there!* Tabatha's car is parked in the smaller lot. I don't believe it. He must have towed it. *Thank God!*

I check the time on my phone and realize it's now after six. Al must have gone home for the day. Either that or he stepped out for a while. I go back to the old man in the booth and ask if Al is around. Luckily, he understands this time and tells me that Al will be back soon. Maybe I can get her car back tonight. Then I won't have to take the bus home.

I tell the old man I'll come back as he nods and says "*Si.*" I'm just glad Tabatha's car wasn't stolen. Now, time to head to the Tower.

In the front of the building, standing around, is a group of rough-looking men. I'd rather not get stopped by them, so instead of crossing the street, I walk halfway down the block and cut in through the alley on the other side.

The alley is dark and dank, and the dumpsters reek of something awful. I get through the fenced-in area and crawl underneath, coming to a back door. I hear the men in front talking. I'm careful not to make much noise, but when I jiggle the handle, I get their attention and they spot me.

"Hey you! Down there, whatchu doin'?" a tall guy with dreadlocks says. The other two follow him. Once they get close, they start messing with me.

"Now look what we got here," the short, heavy one says. "So, what's a pretty little thang like you doin' round these parts?"

All three surround me.

"Look, I'm not here to cause any trouble. I'm just lookin' for some Fix."

"Well, well, well. Why didn't you just say so?" the one with the dreadlocks says. "All you had to do was ask."

The heavy guy reaches in his pocket and pulls out a set of keys.

"Just go to the top floor, apartment 15C, and ask for Big Dog G," the one with the dreadlocks says as the heavy one inserts a key into the door. "And watch out for those crackheads. They'd steal the skin off your back if they could."

"Umm, thanks," I reply, looking back at them as I head inside. My heart is lodged in my throat like a piece of hard candy. And the palms of my hands won't stop sweating. I can't seem to stop this crazy buzzing through my body. The withdrawals from Fix are kickin' in.

The fluorescent lights above me flicker in the halls.

I go straight to the stairway, hearing people as I go. I keep thinking someone's going to jump out at me. This place is so shabby with its thin brick walls. The only thing that's stable is the cement stairs. As I climb up each flight, I'm thinking this is a terrible mistake. Horrible thoughts run through my mind, like I'm going to be raped in a dark room somewhere. Or that I'll get sliced up by some maniac that lives here. It was a lot easier to come here last time, with Fix making me fearless.

Luckily, I'm not stopped by anyone. Other than the chattering in the walls, it's quiet.

Finally, on the top floor, I walk down a graffiti-painted hallway, and notice the door to the rooftop entrance is all gated up. *How am I going to get up there now?* I turn around and look for apartment 15C. The first door on the end is 15G. I must have passed it. I know I've got to be close. Apartment 15C has got to be on this floor. I look at each door— F, E, D, and finally 15C, which is on the other end of the hall.

It only takes a few knocks before someone answers.

"Whatchu want?" a thin, sickly-looking girl wearing a tiny silk robe says, standing in the doorway. Her skin is cracked and dry and her nose is puffy and swollen. She keeps sniffling. Maybe she just snorted up before she answered the door. Judging by the way she looks, I wonder if she's one of Big Dog G's prostitutes.

"I, I'm looking for umm—"

"Well, c'mon now. Out with it!"

"I'm looking for Big Dog G?" I more or less ask instead of say.

"Oh, you 'nother crackhead, aren't you?" She stands there with a smoke in one hand and a bottle in the other. "You lookin' to get fixed up, right?"

"Well, yes. Is he here?"

"He's not back yet. Just have a seat. Wait here." She motions to the torn-up sofa near the window. I hesitate for a second, then enter.

Taking a seat, I look out the window and across the street. I remind myself I need to go back to Al's. That's if I make it out of here.

"You're not just another one of those kids making trouble to see what's up there, are you?" She points straight above her. I'm guessing she's referring to the roof. She looks like someone I go to school with, like just a kid herself.

"Making trouble?" I mumble, trying to get comfortable on the sofa. But I realize that's impossible.

"You haven't heard 'bout them hauntings and shit?" She takes one good look at me, sizing me up and down. "You're not from around here, are you?"

I shake my head.

"Yeah, them hauntings . . . or whatever shit they say." She takes a drag on her cigarette. "Some kids be claiming they saw a ghost. Floatin' around and shit."

My heart sinks deep inside my chest.

"They be sayin' this thing wasn't just no white glow. They be sayin' it was like all colorful and shit, with changing eyes and everything." She pauses for a moment to sit down. I can't help but think of Nate when she says that. The vision of him showing himself to me when we were on the rooftop comes to mind.

"My brother was one of them kids that went up there," she continues. "I know he's been in trouble before and shit like that. But damn, I believe him. He wouldn't lie about somethin' like that." She keeps looking out the windows, her bloodshot eyes reflecting off the glass. "It's a shame you know. The landlord came and chained it all up and never came back. Who knows? Maybe he saw somethin', too." She takes another sip from the bottle and another drag and laughs.

Suddenly, I have the urge to leave. I can't go up to the rooftop to look for Nate now. And I can't help but think this is a sign to get the hell out of here. So, I get up and start walking to the door.

"You know what. Umm, I need to get going. I'll just come back later." I totally lie.

"You don't wanna wait for Big Dog?"

"No. Sorry I bothered you."

I swing the door open and dart down the hallway to the stairwell, flying down the steps. I have this sick feeling Nate had something to do with this. Are other people seeing him? They think he's a ghost. How could Nate possibly be a ghost? That would make him real at one time or another.

Once on the landing, I run out the front doors and straight to Al's to get Tabatha's car.

CHAPTER SEVENTEEN

It feels good to be driving Tabatha's car again. Everything seems to be running fine. I'm almost home now. Al was nice enough to cut me a deal about how much I owed him. He told me he moved it because it was blocking another car. I must have been really stoned when I parked it. He had no way of calling me to tell me.

My mind wanders as I drive. I can't stop thinking about what that girl said back at the Tower. A ghost? The way she described it, it had to be Nate. I remind myself of what Jenelle told me, that years ago I apparently had an "imaginary friend."

I turn down my block and notice blue and red lights bouncing off the houses. There are two cop cars in front of my house. I can only imagine what it must be about. I'm just glad I didn't get high yet. That certainly wouldn't look good to the cops.

I pull into the driveway, get out, and walk to the front. From the side window, two tall, clean-cut men stand with suits on, along with a couple policemen who are talking to my mother. When I walk in, they introduce themselves.

"Penelope Wryter?" the man with gray hair standing on the left says. My mom's off in the corner, wringing her hands together, rocking back and forth.

"Yes?"

"This is Detective Wesson," he motions to the man standing beside him. "And I'm Detective Reeves. We'd like to take you to the police station for questioning."

"For what?" I know this is about Candace. A million things run through my mind. I feel like I'm literally floating around the room, yet my body is still. I can't move. "Did I do something wrong?"

"We just need to go over a few things," Detective Reeves says. He doesn't even look like a detective. With his gray, curly hair, glasses, and big belly, he looks more like someone's grandpa. Maybe he is. "We'd like to take you to the station. It's easier to do the paperwork and fingerprinting there, too."

"Fingerprinting?" If this doesn't make me look shocked, I don't know what will. "Can you at least tell me what this is about?"

"I don't know if you're aware of this or not, but Candace Roman was reported missing last night and our reports show you were one of the people she was with." Reeves pauses for a moment. "Now if you can come with us, we'd appreciate it."

"Penelope, it will be okay. Just listen to them and do what they ask," my mom says. "Call me for a ride or anything at all. I'll be right here for you, honey. Stay strong."

She leans over to me to give me a kiss on the forehead as the detectives guide me out the door. We walk down the sidewalk to the police cars where they squeeze me in the back seat.

For the entire car ride, I'm sweating it out. If they know I was with Candace that night, they must know about Rose's party. What if they already talked to Rose and the others? Christ, I can only imagine what they said. My mind races so much and in this gridlock of questions, I don't even realize when we pull up to the station.

Detective Reeves gets out and opens the door for me. We head inside and I notice a few familiar faces in the waiting area— Rose, Clay, and Walker. They all look at me as I walk past them. Rose seems so stoned that she barely recognizes me. I wonder if the cops will notice she's high. She'd be in a deep world of shit then.

Clay keeps looking around, especially at the small jail cells in the corner. He looks worried. Walker, however, looks straight at me and gives me a reassuring smile, like it's going to be okay. But how the hell does he know that?

The two men guide me into the main office where one of the female police officers takes down some information and my fingerprints. She's somewhat harsh, handling my fingers as if they were popsicle sticks, slapping them on the ink pad. After she's finished, she walks me into an empty room where I am told to wait.

It seems like forever until the two detectives walk back in. The tall, thin Detective Wesson stands over me and doesn't say anything, while Detective Reeves sits down across from me with a file in his hand.

"So, tell me what you know about Candace Roman," he says in a straightforward voice. I sit there for a few minutes thinking of what a bitch she is, but I figure that it wouldn't be a good way to start things out. Instead, I say, "Not much."

"Were you two friends?" Reeves asks.

"Not really."

"Well, were you friends, or not? It's a simple question."

"No. We never really got along."

"Why is that?"

"I don't know. Candace never really liked me, I guess. But Candace didn't like a lot of people."

"And why do you think that is?"

"I suppose she thought she was better than everyone else?"

"You don't seem so sure about that. Is that what you believe?"

"Look, like I said. We weren't really friends."

"But you hung out with the same people?"

"No . . ."

"But our reports say you were with her the night before her disappearance, is that correct?"

That night together flashes across my mind. That horrible high during the Fix circle. The way she hung all over Walker. It was true we were all hangin' out with each other. But in unique circumstances, so I mumble, "That's correct."

"And what was happening at Rose's house?"

I tell him everything I possibly can without it sounding like I'm a total druggie. But then the conversation veers to Fix. Reeves starts asking me questions about the drug—where I get it, how often I do it, how does it make me feel.

I mention Candace didn't seem like the type to get high. I explain that it was her first time and everything. After mentioning to them about the Fix circle, they both look at me with judging eyes. I tell them both exactly what went down, or at least what I remember.

"Don't you understand what a drug like that can do to you?" Reeves asks, edging up his seat to the table. "You realize a drug like that can kill you, right?"

"Yes. I realize that. My sister died from it."

Wesson moves in, hovering over me. "Penelope, tell us exactly what happened."

"I don't know exactly what happened." Aggravation rises inside me. "We all got high in the circle. But when I woke up she was gone. Rose said Justin took her home . . . or halfway home. I don't really know." I start to tremble as cold drifts in—as if some ghost passed right through me. I think of Nate. I don't mention him, I guess so they don't think I'm crazy. I just have this weird feeling he's here with me now.

"Do you know anyone that would want to harm Candace?" Wesson asks.

"No." But that's not true. Half the senior class hates Candace. It could be anyone.

"Listen, if you can think of anything else," Reeves pipes in. "Or you find out more information, please don't hesitate to call." He hands me his business card and gathers the rest of his papers.

The female police officer opens the door as both detectives start to leave. Reeves turns around to mention the session is over and that I am free to leave. He says again if there's anything at all I can remember to please let him know.

I walk back to the waiting room. Walker is still there so I ask him how he's doing. He looks drained and pale, like he may even be getting sick. But he tells me he's all right and that he was waiting for me.

"Let me take you home," he says, standing up. "I have Brian's car."

"And he's okay with that?"

"Yeah, yeah. Don't worry about it. C'mon, let's get out of here."

In the parking lot, Walker beeps the car doors open. I go to the passenger side while he gets in the driver's seat. We pull out and head back home.

We're both silent. I just can't handle talking about it right now.

He takes my hand and looks over to me and smiles—as if trying to tell me that things will be okay. I don't know that. I still have this worrisome feeling that Rose and Clay said something against me.

We pull up to my house and I notice that my mom's car is gone and all the lights are off.

Walker turns to me. "Do you want me to come inside?"

"Yes, I'd like that." I surprise myself by saying that. I'll admit, I miss Walker and the way our relationship used to be. I remember always feeling so calm when I was around him. Well, when we were dating, that is. Seeing him now, comforting me like this, just makes me want to be with him even more.

"C'mon, let's go inside," he says, putting the car in park and getting out. He comes around to my side to open the door.

"Are you sure this is what you want?" I ask, leaning on him as I get out.

"You're the only one I want to be with right now, Pen."

We head into the front room to sit down. He helps me take my coat off and starts rubbing my back a little.

"It will be okay, Pen. They have nothing on us. We did nothing wrong."

"I know." I lean my head on his shoulder, holding his hand tight. He looks at me with his crystal-blue eyes and I know what he wants.

"Sure you want me to stay?" he asks me, cupping my face with his hands. I nod thankfully. He starts kissing my forehead and caressing my shoulders. His lips move down my cheeks and find their way to my lips. Together, we kiss and hold hands. We lay on the couch for a while, caressing each other.

"Are you sure you're okay with this, Pen?" he asks softly as he brushes my hair away from my face.

I look up at him and say, "Yes, I'm sure."

We nestle with each other like two puzzles pieces locking together. His warm skin covers mine and the heat feels amazingly good. As I cradle my head on his chest, feeling his racing heart, he whispers, "I love you."

Hearing those words from him makes my heart flutter fast, as if a small hummingbird is caged inside my chest. As we both lie there, embracing each other, I'm surrounded by comforting warmth. In this moment, I feel safe. My mind wanders off to the first time he said those words to me. We were in his basement, just hanging out together on the couch, listening to alternative music. We were both sophomores and had only been dating for a few months. It was the beginning of the school year and things were getting serious between us. I remember feeling I would just die without him. I was so madly in love. Then when we got too close and I wasn't ready, he pulled back. After he said "I love you" and I didn't say it back, things just hung there.

It wasn't that I didn't love him, I was just scared. I thought we were going too fast. It took so many months to build up the courage to finally tell him, "I love you, too." There was a point in our relationship when I knew he was worried I didn't feel the same. When I finally told him, things started to change and our relationship became rocky from that point on. It's like a switch went off in his mind. Whenever he saw me talking to other guys in the halls, he became viciously jealous. And when Tabatha died, I just snapped.

Looking at him now, lying here with me, I wish we could have the feeling of first falling in love. I think of Nate and how he fits into this equation. I love him so much, but he isn't real.

Walker is.

CHAPTER EIGHTEEN

Walker has left. Images of us together burn in my mind. My body is relaxed and somewhat weak, but I feel good. I can't even process how things will go from here, and whether we'll actually get back together or not. A part of me wants to. And a part of me doesn't. Whatever happens, things will definitely change.

As I lie here thinking, my mind drifts to Nate. I wonder if he'd be upset at me that I'm getting close to Walker again. I desperately want to see him. I want to ask him endless questions. Where did he come from? I won't know unless I get high.

I sit up and glance down the hallway toward Tabatha's room. As always, I have an urge to go in there. I turn the light on and look at all her things. Her bed, neatly made, the dresser off to the side with a few pictures on it. And the black glass urn with purple and pink flowers that holds her ashes. I had it made especially for her. I have every intention to spread her ashes somewhere but I haven't settled on a place yet.

I walk to the dresser, looking at the framed photos of her that my mother propped up along the mirror. She's alone in one, maybe five or six years old, sitting on the sidewalk drawing with chalk. There are a few school pictures. The one of us on the beach together is behind all the other pictures.

I reach to grab it to move it up front, but it slides behind the dresser. *Damn!*

Nestling myself in the corner to move the dresser, I push it sideways and stretch my hand underneath it. The wood boards under her dresser feel loose. I drag the dresser out some more. The picture is lying on the floor. The frame is cracked. Kneeling, I pick it up and slide the photo out. I notice there's something written on the back. It's a phone number that I don't recognize. Whose number could it be? The area code isn't familiar. Who did Tabatha know?

When I kneel to pick up the broken fragments of glass, I notice a plank of wood sticking out from where her dresser was. That must be the piece of wood that's loose. I wobble it back and forth. Is there something under there?

I remove the wooden slab and stick my hand down the small opening, feeling around underneath the boards. There's a hollow space between the floorboards. Some soft installation. Some more thick blocks of wood. Nothing at first. But after reaching in the last corner off to the right, there's something hard and square. It's a box. Quickly, I pull it out and see it's a small pink jewelry box. I remember my father gave it to her as a Christmas present when we were very young. She loved that box. Then it disappeared a few years back—when Tabatha was so lost and drugged up on Fix. She'd always rant about finding that box. Then she'd get quiet for a while. How could I forget how she'd screamed about finding this damn box? And this whole time she had hidden it from herself.

I place the box down, feeling all giddy that I found it. My heart flutters as I wonder what's inside. I run to the door to look down the hallway and stairwell to see if my mom's coming. Once I'm certain the coast is clear, I close the door and take a seat on the bed. Slowly I open the box. A little ballerina pops out and starts dancing as the tune plays. The inside is empty with the exception of a small crumpled napkin. I don't think much of it until I take it out and feel some small, round beads. I place the box down and carefully open the rumpled paper. I'm surprised at what I see—a bunch of little, black, pearl-like pills—Fix.

She stashed Fix. She already had a prescription for that damn depression she had. And to think she was stashing more drugs on the side? I can only imagine how much she was taking. *Damn you Tabatha! Damn you for leaving me!*

I walk back to the small hole in the floor, put back the piece of floorboard, and slide the dresser back into place. I stack the pictures carefully and glance at the picture I had put off to the side. I pick up the remaining shards of glass and throw them into the trash bin by the dresser.

I look at the shiny black pills. *Should I take one now?* Confusion spreads through my mind again. But wanting to see Nate overpowers that. I walk back to the bed, sit down, and pop one in. I put the remaining pills back in the box and stuff it under the bed.

The pill starts to melt under the roof of my mouth. It's like a small bit of saliva until it builds up inside my mouth into a pool of oozing liquid. Only a few seconds pass until I swallow it all down.

The air has changed. It's like my nasal passages were slightly clogged before this and now I can breathe better. Smell more. The scent of dry splitting wood from the floor boards engulfs me—like my nose is up close to an oak tree or something. I go to the window to open it a crack, feeling the cool breeze brush against my face. It's gotten much warmer since the last time I was outside. I hope I will see Nate.

I stand up and little silver shards scatter about. I wonder if I got glass stuck in my eyes, but it doesn't hurt. As I try to shake the spots out of my vision, I begin to hear a faint swishing noise. It sounds like trees swaying in the wind. The noise is coming from within the house. I walk to the door, open it a crack, and listen to the fuzzy noise getting louder. It's coming from downstairs.

I walk down the steps, each one creaking, until I reach the bottom of the stairwell. There's a blue light glowing from the hallway, its light rebounding off the walls.

"Mom? Is that you?" I call out in a whisper, thinking she might have come home. I open the door and see my mom's old junky TV is on static. Scared, my heart pumps, like I just got an electric shock. I reach for the power button to shut it off. With one click, the screen and the fuzzy sound turns off. Just as I'm ready to leave the room, I hear *click, buzz*. The TV flicks back to life.

I shut it off again and take a seat on the edge of the couch.

"What the hell," I say softly.

I'm staring at my reflection in the shiny, mirrored screen when I see something move behind me—a dark figure. Automatically, I think of Nate. Taking a deep breath, I turn around. Nobody is behind me. But when I look back at the TV again I am horrified at what I see. In shock, I stare at the words "help me" written on the screen in a dark, dusty blur. I yell out, "Who are you?"

Again I yell out, "Who the hell are you? Show yourself!"

But not a soul answers me. The room is freakishly quiet. My beating heart thumps through my ears.

I run into the front room, feeling a cold presence pass through me, sending chills throughout my body. I'm spooked. I want to leave.

I go to the kitchen, take my coat, keys, and phone, and start to head for the door.

With a flash, I am reminded of the picture and the unknown phone number. I dare myself to go back into Tabatha's room.

Hurry! Go! Fast!

I sprint back up the stairs and grab the picture lying on the bed and run back down.

I bundle up my coat, take a moment to double-check that I have everything, and leave.

My thoughts zigzag as I drive high, but I keep my eyes on the road. I'm trying not to think of all the weird stuff that's been happening. I wonder if that was Nate back at my house. Does he need my help?

Then my mind switches to Rose, Clay, and Justin. What did they tell the cops? I'm eager to find out more about what really happened during that last circle. Who was behind all that? Could Rose have something to do with it? Those pictures in her room. She was friends with both Candace and Kelly. And both of them are missing. It just seems awfully ironic to me. My mind aches to know if she's involved with this.

I drive down her block, creeping past her house. All the lights are off. The house is completely dark. I know it's after ten already on a Thursday night, but her parents are still not home. Rose never likes to be alone. And I don't see Clay's car either. I don't want to call. I want to see her face-to-face, to actually see if she's lying.

I turn down the main street and head to Clay's house. I want to see for myself what really is going on. Hopefully, she's with him.

CHAPTER NINETEEN

I pull up to Clay's house around 10:30. It's not that late, but I don't want to walk up to the front and knock on the door. Instead, I park the car across the far end of the street and walk down. I'm still pretty high, hearing all these different voices in my head. They're as clear as if someone's standing right next to me, whispering in my ear. Most of them are Rose's voice. The voices play out possible conversations I could have with her. But she's arguing and being defensive with me. It's becoming so distracting, I can't concentrate on what's in front of me.

Suddenly, the air fills with the metallic scent again. I have the taste of blood in my mouth. I bring my hands up to my face, taking a whiff. It's as if I were holding a handful of coins. The steel aroma is strong.

I look around to see if Nate is near. *Don't trust your friends*, his words tangle my thoughts of the days past. As I walk across the street, fighting hard to center myself, a car honks its horn and drives past, splashing water and leaves on me. I'm startled and try to move quick. A gust of wind sends me back, causing me to slip.

I gather myself together, brush off the sticky leaves, and get to the other side of the street. Clay's truck is parked in the driveway. I'm hoping he's here. Looking around, I notice lights on in the basement—Clay's room. Hopefully, he's still up. I don't see why he wouldn't be.

I walk around the house to the backyard, crouch down, and look in the window, peeking through the blinds. He's watching TV. But I don't see Rose. Maybe she's in another room. My heart's thumping so hard, my ears are ready to pop. The thought of confronting Rose doesn't seem worth it. But wanting to know more overrides those feelings as my adrenaline continues to go into overdrive.

After standing there a few minutes in the cool breeze and trying to calm down, I lightly tap on the window a couple of times. Clay sees me and signals to me to hold on, holding up his index finger. He walks into the other room, so I wait.

I look up at the dark sky, so clear and without a cloud. The stars themselves twinkle like small diamonds. I stare so long I can almost see them moving. *Are they moving?* The moon is big and yellow and round and seems to be moving, too. *Man, I'm so stoned.*

As I continue to wait, I trip out on the fall colors. Lots of the trees have already shed their leaves. Piles of them, brown and yellow and red, are littered everywhere, cluttered against the chain-link fence. It's warmer tonight. I watch the dripping awnings create muddy puddles. *C'mon Clay, what's taking you so long?*

My nose starts to run. For a second I'm afraid it's another nosebleed. But after I check, I realize I'm fine. I take a deep breath, holding in my sniffles, and breathe in the scent of fresh earth. The metallic odor has completely gone away. All I smell now is raw dirt.

I wait a few minutes longer until he finally opens the back door and lets me in.

"So, what's going on?" he asks, walking me into the den. Everything is dark except for the glowing TV. There's a card table and chairs off in the corner and a plush sectional in the center with a coffee table in the middle. And a huge flat-screen TV in a wall unit filled with everything you could think of to top it off. *Must be nice that your girlfriend pampers you with her daddy's money.*

I take a seat on the couch while Clay tells me to hold on and walks in the back bedroom. When he returns, he sits down on the couch next to me. That's when I realize I'm a bit uncomfortable knowing it's just me and him. I shouldn't be here like this.

"So, where's Rose?" I ask, squirming a bit. "She around?"

"Oh, she went out with her aunt for dinner. But she's on her way now." He smiles. "You know Rose. She can't stand being alone in that huge house of hers."

He scoots himself closer to me, making me feel even more uncomfortable. *Why is he sitting so close?*

"Walker and Justin are talking about coming over, too. We were thinking of just hangin' out for a while. Glad you're here. Take your coat off . . . stay a while."

"Umm, I don't really think that's a good idea. I'm just looking for Rose. You know when she'll be back?"

He inches in closer and puts his arms around the top cushions, right above my shoulders.

"Not sure. Why, what's up with you?"

He pulls at my arm for a second, nudging me to take my coat off. Don't ask me why, but I do. I guess I'm hoping to get more comfortable. Maybe kill a few seconds while we wait. Like it's going to make a big difference.

Time passes, five minutes, maybe more, without us

saying a word. The ticking of the clock on the wall is so loud it sounds like an annoying insect. Again, in my head, the fighting with Rose starts. *What the hell are you up to? What are you hiding from me?* I'm asking her. Inside my mind, she's arguing with me. She's pissed. *You shouldn't be here,* she's saying.

Clay and I begin to watch TV. Everything seems okay except for my inner turmoil, until Clay turns to me and tells me how pretty I look tonight. A red flag right there. I think of the time we were in the car alone together and how he made a pass at me. When he starts playing with my hair, I back off and swat at his hand.

"What the hell are you doing, Clay?"

He smiles and says nothing. Just as he leans in to kiss me, I hear the knob to the back door jiggle.

"Did you hear that? Someone's coming," I tell him but he ignores me. "Clay? What the hell?" I keep swatting at him. "That could be Rose!"

He mumbles, "It's nothing." I'm beginning to think Clay lied to me. Maybe it's someone else. Why he's totally ignoring it is beyond me. He seems in a zone. As I continue to inch away, Clay continues to lean in closer. "Clay, stop!" I try to push him off. He gets aggressive and starts holding my head on the cushions, pressing his lips onto mine. Before I can try to push him off, Walker comes in through the back door.

"What the hell!" Walker shouts out in shock. "God, Penelope! Again with this shit?"

Walker starts shooting off his mouth, walking closer to Clay like he's ready to jump on him. Clay pops up and holds his hands in the air like he got busted by the cops. "Walker, we weren't doing anything. Please don't tell Rose!"

I quickly grab my coat and start walking toward the back door.

I look over to Walker and say, "I'm sorry. I just . . . I just can't take this shit right now."

"Thanks a lot, Penelope. It would be like you to just leave."

For a split-second I want to tell him how wrong he is. That it wasn't my fault. That Clay was the one that was coming on to me—attacking me. But Walker wouldn't believe me. He didn't believe me about Justin, why would he believe me now? So instead of explaining myself, I let them work it out and turn around to leave.

I race back to my car, get in, and slam the door shut. For a moment or so, I sit there trying to unscramble my mind. It's so intertwined, I can't think straight. I'm praying Walker won't say anything to Rose about what just happened. The last thing I need is for her to be pissed off at me. Then I will never find out anything.

As I sit collecting my thoughts, the picture in the front compartment starts to glow. I don't know if I'm imagining things or it's because I'm still high, but I reach over and pick it up. I flip the picture over and stare at the numbers. At first, they change, mix, and garble out of order. I look up and try to shake off the dizziness.

When I look back, my motion sickness stops and I'm able to focus. When I start up the car, I dare myself to call the number.

I take out my phone, rolling it around in my hand, debating. Finally, after taking a deep breath, I dial the number—slowly. I get to the last digit and press send, putting the phone up to my ear. I'm ready to hang up, but before I do, a man answers.

"Hello?" he says in a low voice. I want to keep quiet, but I'm so rattled I almost start speaking. It's on the tip of my tongue to ask him who he is. Yet I hold back.

"Hello? Who is this?" he says again. A second or two goes by, and I chicken out and hang up.

I exhale with a deep sighing breath. *Man, I can just about throw up.* I don't know if it's because Fix is now starting to wear off or it's because of this psycho day I've had.

I press my forehead against the steering wheel, thinking of the voice over and over. It sounded like an older man. But who could it be? Why would Tabatha have his number written down on the back of this picture? Could it be someone she was dating just before she died that I didn't know about?

I shouldn't be sitting here like this. Walker or Clay could come out at any minute looking for me. In a way, I'm surprised Walker didn't follow me. A part of me wanted him to. This really wasn't my fault. Before I put the car into drive, I check down the block and over to Clay's house again, but nothing. *This is crazy! I gotta get out of here!* I start the car and head home.

CHAPTER TWENTY

I wake up and instantly my head starts to throb. My mom ditched me last night. She told me she'd be home when I got back from the police station. She hasn't even asked me what's going on. I think she's too wrapped up with Ken right now to even see that her daughter is in distress. You'd think she'd be more concerned after what happened to Tabatha.

The remaining pills I tucked away under Tabatha's bed come to mind. I can almost hear them calling me. Getting ready as quickly as I can, I lay my clothes out for the day and hop in the shower, not even letting the water warm up first.

I quickly wash my hair and body and rinse off. I wrap a towel around my wet body, still thinking of those pills. The last time I got high, I didn't see Nate. I'm wondering if the message in the TV screen was him trying to contact me. Maybe he needs my help. I don't know. But the urge to take Fix again is overwhelming.

After I get dressed and comb my hair, I slap on some mascara and brush my teeth. The same wave of thoughts continues to flow through my mind. What if this? What if that? I keep thinking if I take Fix again, I'll see him. Or perhaps if I will Nate to appear, mentally chanting his name, it will happen. Enough rationalizing on the whys and why nots, I finally decide. I'm taking another one. There's too much crap going on not to. What do I have to lose?

Back in Tabatha's room, I crouch down and reach for the jewelry box. It's right where I left it. I open it and unravel the napkin. The black pills nestle in the middle. I pluck one out.

I shove the box back, and head into the bathroom and tear off a piece of toilet paper to wrap the pill in. I don't want to take it just yet. Instead, I carefully place it in the small pocket of my jeans.

Before I leave for school, I check on my mother. She's sprawled out on her bed, snoring away. I didn't even hear her come in last night. This thing with Ken is escalating. I don't know if they're fighting or something happened between them or what. She isn't telling me. But he seems to be her only priority now.

I close the door softly and head out.

I park Tabatha's car down the street from the school and walk the rest of the way. As I make my way toward the school, I reach into in the small pocket, and with a pinching motion, take the rolled-up ball of toilet paper out, and reveal the pill. I pop it in my mouth like it's a piece of candy.

Like magic, the pill starts kicking in. First, there's the wave of nausea, yet I always seem to hold it in. Most of the time, at least. Then, as my mood takes over, I adjust the hue of the day. Even though it's still unseasonably warm, it's grey and overcast. I watch the sky turn as if God is mixing paints above me. The swirls of grey suddenly disappear, pooling into a pale blue as the sun creeps over the open land to the eastside. It's peering through the brittle branches and making the ground golden. In this moment, I feel good. I am confident that if I think about Nate hard enough, he will appear.

As I approach a crowd of kids, I notice something form between two school girls huddling together, wearing burkas. At first, all I can see are the girls, robed in black from head to toe. But as they begin to separate, a dark shadow forms between them. There's a distant energy, like some far away heat. It is as if I am standing near a fire. The dark shadow forms into Nate. He's between the two girls with his back turned and hood up. I know it's him. I just need him to turn around. To face me. He's got to know I'm here.

I speed up, walking faster until I am a few yards behind them. They reach the school entrance and the girls walk in, followed by Nate. For a split second, he turns back to look me in the eye. His silver eyes zap me with a cold chill. The hairs on my arms stand up as goose bumps bubble up on my skin. The door closes behind him, and just like that, he's gone.

I get frustrated and confused, watching the sky turn into a weird green, like it's ready to swirl into a tornado. I wonder, because my mood's changing so much, if I'm the one making the sky turn. I try to remind myself that it's not real. It's just what I'm seeing. But the threatening sky is still disturbing.

As I fight my way through the halls, I see distinct, long, yellow hair from a few yards away. I am drawn to it, thinking it can only be one person. Instead of going straight to class, I follow her. It seems like she's gliding rather than walking— it's eerie. I want her to turn around. I get chills just looking at her. Once she gets to the end of the hall, she turns into the bathroom, and looks right at me. *It's her.* Candace. But she looks so pale.

I follow her, but once I get into the bathroom, she's gone. I look in all the stalls, nothing. *Where did she go?* I glance in the mirror, startled to see her standing right behind me. She silently mouths, "help me." When I turn around, there's nothing there. *I must be seeing things.*

I close my eyes for a moment to clear my head. I need to get to class.

In homeroom, Walker is sitting at his desk, talking to another student. When he sees me, he gets quiet. I wonder if he knows I'm high. I am freaked out after seeing Candace. I'm so shaken up about things, he probably can't tell I'm stoned. I try to shake the weird feeling off, but I can't help but look at him. He seems so sad. I have the urge to talk to him and explain that it wasn't my fault. I swallow all my worrisome thoughts and walk over to his desk.

"Walker, I need to talk to you about last night."

"There's no need."

"What is that supposed to mean?" I give him a puzzled look. I wonder what Clay had said.

"Don't worry, I'm not going to tell Rose. Whatever you do with whoever is fine. We're not going out anymore."

"But it's not my fault! You have to believe me." My eyes begin to water and as I look out the windows, it starts to rain. I don't know if it's raining for sure, or if I am making it happen. He looks at me strangely, eyeing me up, down, and sideways and back into my eyes again.

"You're high, aren't you?" he accuses me.

"Please, can we just talk about this?"

"You're seeing Nate again, aren't you?" He stands up and looks out the window, too. "So, where is he this time?"

He has me stumped for a moment. I don't know where Nate is.

"Nate's not real," he continues. "When are you going to accept that?"

There's an awkward pause between us before he says, "You need help, Pen."

"Oh, I need help? You should talk! You get high, too!" I snap.

"Not anymore. I'm done with that shit."

Before I can say more, the bell rings and the teacher tells everyone to sit down. I'm surprised Walker is quitting. I hope he knows it's harder than it seems.

The day passes as normal. One by one, students walk like drones to each of their classes. Hours have gone by, but it feels like an eternity. I want to get out of here so badly. I'm hoping to talk to Jenelle about all this. I need someone to talk to. I can't take this anymore. She's the only one I can think of who might listen.

While walking to my last class, a light goes on in my head. I'm starting to think about that phone number and the guy who answered. Fix has now worn off. And I haven't seen any more weird sightings of Candace either. I can at least think a little more clearly now. I want to go to the library instead and use the computers again. Maybe I can find an address to that number online.

The entire day went by without seeing Rose or the guys. I'm kinda glad I haven't run into Clay. But Rose, on the other hand, I worry about. Down the hall I hear laughter. That same familiar laugh I've heard for four years straight. It's high-pitched and annoying. As the crowd of people clears out, my assumptions are right. It's Rose.

I don't rush over to her. I'm far enough away that she doesn't see me. She's at the corner of the hall talking to someone. I assume it's Clay. But when the person steps around the corner and into the hallway, I'm a bit surprised who it is—Justin.

I get a little closer, standing outside the library doors, but keep my distance so they don't see me. Justin's saying something, something, ". . . forget about them."

Rose is laughing the whole time and getting close to him. Normally, I wouldn't think twice about all the flirting she's doing with him. But when she lifts her arms, I notice something oddly familiar twinkling in the light. The reflection off her wrist sparkles. When I squint my eyes into focus, I'm horrified at what I see. Jiggling on Rose's wrist is Candace's charm bracelet. The last time I saw it, Candace was wearing it at the party. Right before she disappeared.

My mind scrambles. Why would Rose have it? Could Candace have given it to her for some reason? Maybe Candace dropped it? Rose was with her the night she disappeared. But if she did something, what motive would she have? I think of the vision of Candace in the bathroom mirror and shiver.

The bell rings and everyone clears out of the halls. I go into the library and head to the computers. I try to calm my nerves and concentrate on focusing on the number. I want to know why Tabatha wrote down this old guy's number and how she knew him.

After I sign in, I immediately open Internet Explorer and type the number on the Google command line. A ton of links pop up. I choose the first one, obtaining an address that's just on the outskirts of town. It's got to be it. It's the exact phone number. After I get out of here, I plan to drive by the address and see for myself who this person is.

CHAPTER
TWENTY-ONE

Before I head over to this guy's house, Jenelle texts me, wanting to meet at the mall. Since she's my only friend right now, I don't want to turn her down, so I agree. I drive to the mall and wait for her in the food court. We usually meet somewhere public like this. She used to come over to my house a lot when we were younger, but I rarely went to hers. I can only recall one or two times being there. She had a family party years ago, but I don't remember it much. All I remember was meeting her mother, but not her dad. We became friends after her parents divorced. *When was it? Kindergarten or first grade?*

Soon after her parents divorced, her mother remarried, and I don't remember seeing her stepfather. Jenelle always talked about her stepbrothers and sisters. I think I met them when I was little a few times, though if I were to pass them on the street I wouldn't recognize them.

I check the time on my phone and realize half an hour has passed. As I gaze around the food court looking for Jenelle, that same eerie chill I had in school when I saw Candace creeps over me. Looking across the array of tables, a cool draft wafts out of nowhere and blows at my feet. I sense someone, or something, standing in front of the Pizza Hut line. When the crowd clears, my eyes lock onto a teenage girl. Her back is turned toward me. There's a weird glow about her. Her image is fuzzy, blurred-like, but everything else in the food court is crystal clear. When she turns around, I'm stunned at who it is. With her dark brown hair, light eyes, and that unmistakable porcelain skin, it's Kelly—the missing girl. But how the hell can that be? How can I be having this vision sober?

I squint my eyes and try to focus. She's whispering something repeatedly. I can make out her mouthing a word and then "me." Oh, my God. She's whispering, "help me." I rub my eyes and stand up for a better view. All the blood rushes to my head and the room starts to spin, so I sit back down. The vision fades and the coolness evaporates—and so does Kelly.

I'm sick of seeing people who aren't there. It's as if I'm high, but I'm not. At least if I was stoned, I could say it's because of the drug, but now I don't know. I don't know anything anymore.

I try to focus and keep an eye out for Jenelle and ignore everything else. I'm so freaked out right now, my body won't stop shaking. I drop my head down, too scared to look up anymore. I don't want to see Candace, or Kelly. I don't even want to see Nate right now. I hate not knowing what's real and what's not. Jesus Christ, it's like I've developed some mental disorder or something.

I take a few deep breaths and try to calm down, wondering what's keeping Jenelle. Sitting at a table in the corner between Panda Express and Taco Bell, the smells of hot and spicy Chinese food and warm cheesy tacos linger. I watch the workers pressing the shells in the steamer and squirting sour cream on the food. I'm starting to get hungry and debate ordering something when I see Jenelle coming through the sliding glass doors. She smiles and waves, letting me know she spots me.

"I'm sorry I'm late. I had to run an errand for my mom."
She slides out the thin metal chair and sits down.

"How is your mom, anyway?"

"Good, considering all that's happened." She takes her
coat off to get comfortable.

"Why, what's going on?"

"Oh, the divorce, I didn't tell you?"

"No, you mean again?" I give her a puzzled look.

"Oh, yeah . . . again. My stepdad moved out a few years
back and now after all this time, he gives her divorce papers.
I still keep in touch with his side of the family though." Some
loose red curls fall off her shoulders and her pretty green
eyes almost glow in the light from the skylights.

"Oh, I'm sorry to hear that, Jenelle. I didn't know."

"It's okay. I'm used to it. So, tell me what's going on
with you?"

"I don't know, Jenelle. Some really weird shit's been
happening to me lately. It's kind of hard to explain. And this
stuff with Rosario, I don't know where to start." My words trail
off as I look back to the sliding glass doors as if someone's
going to magically appear, like Nate or Candace, but nothing.

"I told you she was bad news," Jenelle says, giving me
a stern look. "Just start from the beginning. I'm willing to
listen to whatever you have to say."

"Thank you," I say with a sigh. "This is nice. It helps to
talk about it."

Since I basically have no one else to really talk to, I tell
her everything that's on my mind. I tell her about how Rose,
who is supposed to be my best friend, seems to flirt with
every guy, yet she is with Clay. How she urges me to take
Fix and how something seems to be off with her lately. I go

on to tell her about the Fix circle and finally confide in her about Nate and my sightings of the missing girls. Jenelle gives me a concerned look. She says being on drugs, of course, doesn't help.

"I saw something on the local news about Kelly the other day," she says. "I can't believe they still haven't found her. And Candace, too? Wow . . . it's just so horrible."

Jenelle's always been a good listener. She lets me pour my heart out about everything. I even talk about Tabatha a bit and how my mom is too friggin' stupid to see that her jerk boyfriend is a loser. I tell her how I miss my mom a lot and wish things could be different.

"I know it must be hard for you, Pen. You know I am always here for you if you need it," she says with a sympathetic smile. I smile back to show my thanks. "You know what you should do," she says. "Just put this all behind you, stop taking that damn Fix. You'd enjoy life more."

I wonder how that is even possible.

"You know what you need, Pen?"

"What?" I hope she doesn't say I need help, like Walker did.

"You need a boyfriend." Her words surprise me. "We could go boy hunting. You know, Jared's the best thing that happened to me. I've had a hard time, too."

I nod my head in agreement.

"I have an idea," she says, looking like she has a secret to tell me. "We should all go to that dance at your school."

I shake my head thinking, no, not a good idea.

But Jenelle keeps talking it up.

I grimace. "But what about Rose?" I ask, even though I'm not sure I'd want her to come. "I thought you didn't like her."

"Oh, that was all in the past!" she waves me off. "Come on, it'll be fun."

"You know, Jared stopped me in the hall," I add. "He gave me extra tickets, too."

"Perfect! There you go. You can ask Walker to come, too. Maybe things will get better between you guys."

"Yeah, I guess."

It's doesn't seem all that bad. Maybe that's what I need. A fun night out? Perhaps to turn things around.

I tell her that sounds like a good idea and that maybe I'll bring it up to Rose and my other friends. I think of asking Walker. Maybe I can get him to stop hating me. I suppose it's worth a shot.

I leave the mall and head to the parking lot. The whole time I'm thinking that Jenelle has a point. Maybe I am overanalyzing things too much and should just relax. And just quit Fix all together. Ha. Easier said than done.

Going to the dance does sound like a positive and healthy way to have fun. I wonder if inviting Rose would be a good idea. I still think she's full of secrets. I don't trust her.

But once I get to the car, my attitude changes when I see the picture again. I left it lying in the middle compartment tray. I look at it again, concentrating on the image of Tabatha, then turn it over to see the phone number written in Tabatha's handwriting. I *was* planning on going there next, but now I second-guess myself. I have the address. I *should* go.

Several minutes pass. Just as I'm ready head over, my phone rings.

It's Rose.

My heart nearly jumps out of my mouth. I still think she knows something I don't. There's only one way to find out. On the fourth ring I answer.

"Hey, you, what are you doing?" She sounds in good spirits, like she doesn't know what happened between me and Clay the other night. "Hello? You there?" She gets annoyed I don't answer right away. "Penelope!"

"Yeah, yeah, I'm here."

"Good. So, we're going out tonight. Come with us."

"Where to?"

"Ryan's Woods," she says in a whisper, like it's some big secret. I haven't been there since I went with Walker back when we were dating. And I really don't want to go to the forest preserve late at night and get all bit up by mosquitos, but Rose sounds so excited. Maybe I'm overreacting. Maybe it will be fun.

"Okay, I'll go."

Rose seems all pumped I said yes. She's eager to party. As she rambles on about getting Fix for tonight, I think of asking her about the dance, but decide to wait.

After we end our phone conversation, I look at the picture and address again. Whoever it is, they live only a few streets west from here. I could be there in about fifteen minutes. I back out of the parking lot and turn west on the main street, heading toward the address.

I pump up the music in the car to try and clear my mind. It works for the moment. I feel a little better. I am glad I visited Jenelle. Even though she doesn't relate to the drug scene or my friends, it is good to talk to her. Maybe I could slowly wean myself off Fix if I was around someone who wasn't using. I could get healthy again.

I pull up to the house around 5:30. It's a pretty nice house—a big old Cape Cod with triangular peaks and everything. It's already dark, and whoever is home has all the lights on and the curtains slightly open.

I want to knock on the door and talk to this guy, but what would I say? "Hi, I found your phone number on the back of my dead sister's photo." *Yeah, like that's gonna work.* I need a good reason.

As I watch from inside the car, I can tell someone's home. Probably the old man. I'm parked far enough away that he wouldn't be able to see me. But I can tell that he's walking back and forth in the front room. I see him sit down and start to read a book. I wonder how old he is. From the looks of his receding brown hair and his thick, husky build, he could be in his late forties, maybe early fifties? As I am deliberating whether or not to approach the house, my phone dies. Then I have an idea. I get out and slowly walk to the front door. My heart is beating a mile a minute and my palms begin to sweat. *Okay, just keep it cool, Pen.*

I take a deep breath and ring the doorbell. He looks through the side window and comes to the door.

"Yes, can I help you?"

"Yeah, umm, I'm hoping you can. I'm lost and my phone just died. This area is pretty dark and I saw that your lights were on . . ." my voice trails off.

"Sure, where do you need to go?" He has the door open a crack.

"Well, umm, I need to go to Orland Park," a random suburb that just popped in my head.

"Sure, absolutely, you can take . . ." His house phone begins to ring as he is about to answer me. "Oh, can you hold on a minute?"

"Sure."

He leaves the door wide open as he goes to answer the phone. I'm surprised he is being so trusting. I guess I am coming across as believable.

I look into the house as I stand in the doorway. The front room is homey looking. There's a grand piano with pictures of his family of all different sizes on top, and some really expensive-looking furniture. As my eyes travel around the room, I catch sight of something. When I glance back to the pictures on the piano, my heart lurches to the pit of my stomach.

It can't be, can it?

Feeling nauseous and unsure, I keep looking at the picture as if it is going to change. But it doesn't. That hair, that chiseled jawline. Those unmistakable eyes. Suddenly, I feel dizzy as everything starts to spin. I place my hand on the doorframe to regain my balance.

When I look back at the picture, it is as clear as day.

It's Nate.

My Nate.

My heart races so fast my cheeks flare up with heat. I want to leave, but the man hasn't come back yet. I wait a few minutes more, looking away from the piano and the picture and out to the street. I don't think I can bear to see another inch of this place.

The man comes back and instructs me how to get to Orland Park, even though I know full well how to get there.

And then it happens. I hear the words come out before I can stop it. I have to know.

"Who is that guy in the picture? Is he your son?" I point to the piano. I shiver with nervousness.

"Yes, it is," he says. "Are you okay?"

"Yes, sorry to bother you. I'm sorry to ask this, but is your son home?"

I just have to know. I must.

"Are you one of his friends?" he asks, giving me this weird look, furrowing his eyebrows.

"Yes," I lie. "I went to school with him."

His face drops and he looks down for a moment. "I'm sorry to tell you this, but my son passed away about a year ago. Was he close to you?"

"Oh, umm . . . no, not really. I just . . . umm," my words come out garbled. "I just, I'm really sorry to bother you. Thank you for the information."

"Oh, it's okay. I have teenagers myself. I wouldn't want any of them getting lost. Glad to help."

I thank him again and go straight back to the car. But in my mind, I am exploding. I barely manage to pull away. I am flooded with questions. If Nate was once a living, breathing person, what is he now? A ghost? Why does he appear to me? And most importantly, how did Tabatha know him?

CHAPTER TWENTY-TWO

I pull up in the driveway, and see that my mom is home from work early. It seems we've been missing each other lately, like two ships passing in the night. I have the urge to talk to her about Tabatha. My mom must know something. Granted, I was close to my sister, but come to think of it, we always talked about my problems. Tabatha always focused on me, which I loved. But I took advantage of that, never really realizing how she truly felt and what was going on in her life. I would ask, of course, but Tabatha was always great for skirting around the issues. She never confronted them head on. I used to be that way before Fix. Now it's so different. I almost know why she never wanted to say much of anything. Maybe it was too complicated for her to deal with, so she escaped to get high to avoid it all. Kind of how I am now.

It's nearly seven o'clock and the kitchen smells of peppers, onions, and spicy chicken fajita. Ordinarily, I would be interested in eating, but I'm not really hungry. She probably isn't even making it for me anyway.

My mom comes from around the corner and into the kitchen. "Oh, hey, you're home. I was just making dinner for me and Ken. He's sleeping right now, but when he gets up, it should all be done. Want some?" She stirs the meat around, wiping her hands on a small dish towel hanging on the handle of the stove door. She never asked me why the cops came by to get me. I know my mom likes to avoid confrontation, but to not ask at all seems neglectful.

"No, I ate already." I lie. "Thanks anyway." I take a seat at the kitchen table as silence lingers between us with the exception of the sizzling food on the stove. I'm sick of dancing around and not connecting with her. There's so much of Tabatha's death I don't understand. And I still miss my dad, too. Instead of going to my room, I open up to her, trying to lead up to the real questions I want to ask.

"Mom?"

"Yeah, what is it, honey?"

"Do you miss them?"

She doesn't say anything for a while. She has her back turned to me and is concentrating on the food. For a moment, I wonder if she heard me.

"I miss them all the time," she says, then stops. I'm waiting for her to say more but she doesn't.

I continue to prod. "What do you miss most?"

"The little things." She continues to stir the mixture simmering on the stovetop. "Like when Tabatha would fix her hair in the bathroom. Remember how she'd spray her hair for hours it seemed? And that sweet smell would linger all throughout the house?"

"Yeah, I do."

"That's what I miss. Her smell . . . and everything else."

"What about Dad?"

"Oh, ha!" she laughs and finally turns around. "I don't know where to begin. You know, I always would kid him about having the remote. And when he couldn't find it, he would feverishly look around the house for it. He'd carry that thing around everywhere." She stands there and sighs, holding the spoon and thinking to herself. She really is a beautiful woman. She looks so much like my sister and I, long golden-blonde hair and striking blue eyes. She always kept a slim figure, too. Just now she lets a bit too much hang out in the front, if you know what I mean.

"I keep those remotes all over the house, just hoping he'll find them. You know, to see if they'd move or disappear. Like he is still here looking for them. I know it's corny, but still."

The food is sizzling and smoking on the stove, but she doesn't take notice. I think I got her thinking good memories of my dad. It's good to see. I don't want to ruin it for her. It makes me feel as though she still loves him. And, in a way, I know she does.

"What about Tabatha?"

"What about her? She was remarkable. But I don't have to tell you that."

"I know, but I feel like there are things I don't know about her. I keep finding stuff around the house that reminds me, and I think why this and why that? You know?"

"Yeah, but all that's normal," she says with a sigh. "I go through that, too. I even get angry and frustrated over what she did sometimes. Then I think of all the times she seemed so happy."

The food continues to sizzle, but I don't care if it gets burnt. It's for that jerk anyway. I continue to ask her questions. "Did she have someone?"

"Someone? What do you mean, like a boyfriend?"

"Yeah. I mean, I know she dated and stuff, but there's got to be more to it."

"She had a friend at her work. She'd come home complaining about being on the register at Kmart. I know she hated it toward the end. But there was this one guy she mentioned quite a bit."

"Do you remember his name?"

"Not sure, I would have to think on it more."

The chicken is sizzling and creating heavy smoke, so I tell her she should check on the food. She turns around with surprise that she let the food go unattended as long as it did.

"Oh, no, I think I burned it." She turns the burners off and waves the smoke out to clear the air as it travels quickly into the other rooms, setting the smoke detectors off.

"What the fuck, Sharon!" Ken comes stumbling in the kitchen. "You burned my dinner?"

I get up from the table and make some smartass remark, playing on his every last nerve. He gets even more upset and starts yelling at the top of his lungs. So many nasty things come out of his mouth, he doesn't even make any sense. Even after his nap, he is still drunk.

"Sharon, you're just worthless," he slurs out, checking the blackened food. He starts shaking her violently, catching me off guard.

"Ken! Get your hands off her, or I'll call the cops," I yell out. He swings his arm out and backslaps me into the corner.

"You prick!" my mother spits out at him. "Get out! Just get out!"

"My pleasure. You and your dumbass daughter can have each other."

He takes his coat and storms out the back door.

I debate whether or not to go to the Kmart where Tabatha worked. The idea that Nate may have worked with her makes me want to talk to someone there. I don't want to go back to his father's house. That would be too eerie. And I think that would be disrespectful to him, too—and all around uncomfortable. But I realize it's getting late and I still need to get ready if I want to go out with Rose and everyone else tonight.

My mom has been quiet since the incident with Ken. Maybe she is finally realizing things are bad. He's a jerk and brings nothing to the relationship. He sucks the life out of her. When we spoke earlier, I saw a glimmer of hope—that things could be different. Now she's in her room with the door closed, sulking. I just hope she dumps him. She doesn't need that headache. And neither do I.

I take a quick shower and get dressed. Rose calls to let me know they are on their way. I hurry up with my makeup and blow-dry my hair. Soon, I hear them pull up in the driveway and honk the horn. I go to the window and hold my finger up to let them know I'll be right out. They're all crammed in Justin's car. From here, I see Rose is in the front passenger side and Walker in the back. Clay must be in the back, too, as Justin is driving.

I grab my phone and extra cash just in case I need it. I run downstairs and out the front door.

"Yo, girl, what up?" Rose says, turning around from the front. "You can squeeze in the back with the boys."

Walker slides to the middle, making room for me. I can't tell by the look on his face if he's still mad at me. Maybe he thinks I shouldn't be out partying. He said he was quitting Fix. But he's here with us, too, so it's not like he isn't partying at all. He should talk.

Even though it's loud in the car with the music pumping, everyone's having different conversations. Walker turns to me and mentions he wants to talk to me later. I figure it has something to do with the Clay incident. Maybe he wants me to tell Rose what happened.

We get to the forest preserve at around ten. We park just a block or so off the main street. Everything is super dark.

Everyone gets out. Clay and Justin grab the cooler from the back. After Rose snatches blankets from the trunk, she catches up to them. They're already a few yards ahead. I figure we're hiking up to the campsite that we usually go to.

"Come on you guys, hurry up," Rose yells out. Walker continues to linger. I suppose he wants to talk.

"Hey, how you doing?" he asks, walking beside me.

"Okay, I guess." Not really though.

"Mind if we talk for a bit?" He gives me an inviting smile. "I want to apologize for that thing that . . ."

"You don't have to," I say, cutting him off before he could say it. "It's over now."

"Yeah, but seriously though, Penelope. It really isn't my business. It's not like we're going out. I mean, I know we got close again the other night, but that doesn't mean we're together."

"Listen, that thing that happened between me and Clay?"

"Yeah?"

"Well, it wasn't like I wanted that. He was forcing himself on me. It wasn't my fault. You actually walked in at a good time." I look at him with sincerity. "I just want you to know that, okay?"

"Yeah, well, I figured that. Before we got here, Clay attempted to tell me what happened, and I put two and two together. What Clay did pissed me off. We're going to have a serious talk later."

"No! Don't!" I spurt out. "Just let it rest for a while. I still need to talk to Rose."

Walker hesitates in silence for a moment. "Fine, but if he ever does that shit again—"

"Yeah, I'll let you know."

"Promise?"

"Promise." We continue to walk side by side.

"So, can we call this a truce, then?" he asks, smiling.

"I guess you can say that."

He gives me a wider smile. "You know, I wouldn't mind giving it another run."

I stop walking and look at him. "Oh, you mean doing it again?"

"No, Penelope," he says, stopping me as we walk through the field. "I want us to be together again. I'd like to give it another try."

My heart speeds up. I'm caught in a tight spot right now. I really haven't given much thought to this until now. It's overwhelming. Thoughts of Nate and Walker wrestle in my mind.

"Listen, you don't have to say anything now. Just promise me you'll think about it?"

"Sure."

As we start to walk again, I think of all the times Walker and I came to these very woods—just me and him. All the times we sat by the brook underneath the viaduct and talked. There were so many things we'd say to each other, it was like we were an old couple and had been married for years. We had intimate talks back then. Like when his mother passed away from lung cancer, he used to write letters to her. Some of the letters he wrote to her, he shared with me right here.

Sometimes he'd write letters just for me and read them to me while we sat under the large willow trees. I miss his letter writing. I still have every single one.

I quickly realize Rose, Clay, and Justin are gone. How did they get so far ahead of us?

I look to Walker and ask if he sees the rest of the group. He shakes his head.

"Rose? Clay?" I call out. "Where are you guys?"

"Just stay close, Pen. We'll catch up to them soon," Walker tells me. But I can see the concerned look in his eyes.

"Rosario, where the hell are you?" I'm getting slightly annoyed now. Like, not this shit again.

"Hello out there!" Walker screams. He looks at me and shakes his head.

"Let's keep looking," I tell him. The crickets buzz, filling the deadening silence.

At the end of the clearing, Walker and I go into the woods.

"They must be playing a prank or something," he says. It's getting darker.

"They have to be around here somewhere, come on." I'm disgusted at this point.

"You take that side and I'll check around there," Walker says, pointing to the other side of the woods. "Just stay close."

While Walker searches to the right of me, I search to the left. As I walk, I hear the trickling of water close by. There must be a creek near here. The temperature drops a bit while I walk farther in and toward the creek. It's so dark that it's hard to tell what's what. The leaves are black, the trees are black, everything is black.

As Walker and I call out to the others, I come to the

creek. The moonlight casts light across the glimmering water. My eyes travel across the stream until I see something floating along the rocks. It looks like one of the blankets Rose was carrying. Wading across the cool water to take a closer look, I see that it's a piece of clothing caught under a log. I wonder if someone lost their jacket. When I go to fish it out with a stick, I flip it over and gasp in horror. It's a body. And from the rotting, waterlogged face, and long yellow hair drifting along the surface, it could only be one person.

CHAPTER TWENTY-THREE

"Walker!" I scream out. "Walker, hurry!"

Walker comes rushing to my aid within seconds. "What? What is it?"

I point to the body.

"Jesus Christ!" he belts out. "We have to call the police."

Just then, Rose, Clay, and Justin come running over.

"God, Pen, can't you take a joke," Rose says, trying to catch her breath. "We were only playing around."

She looks over to the dead body and her face drops. "Holy shit!" Rose cups her hands to her mouth. Clay and Justin are silent and staring in disbelief. There's a deep gaping wound on the dead girl's neck, her eyes stare upward, the life from them all but gone.

Walker pulls out his phone to call the police.

"Ask for Detective Reeves," I tell him. He nods.

Rose clicks her tongue. "Well, there goes partying tonight."

I'm troubled by her comment. But maybe she's just in shock. Clay and Justin stand there, horrified.

Within minutes the police arrive.

I sleep away half of the next day. When I wake, I'm safe and back at home in my room. It should be comforting, but I'm too shaken. I start trying to prepare myself for the dance later on tonight and forget about last night. But it's impossible. My body trembles as I wade through my closet, picking out something to wear. I choose a black party dress and hang it on the door.

Rumors have already started to fly that it was Candace. And from what I saw, I'm sure it was. I can't get the image out of my mind. It looked like she was eaten by some kind of animal after she died. And those eyes, so light and pale. Normally, her eyes were a colorful blue, but not last night. All the life inside of her was gone.

I scroll through the messages on my phone from last night, trying to catch my breath. I can't stop my heart from beating so wildly in my chest.

I look at Rose's last text. She kept telling me it will be okay. It seemed like she was bummed out that we couldn't party. Then again, Rose's reactions to things are always skewed when she's high on Fix. And she is *always* high. If the cops hadn't called us in for questioning again, she probably would have continued to party.

Walker was more shocked than anyone else. He kept saying that he should have never taken Candace to the party. He kept blaming himself.

As I try to clean my room up, I keep glancing at the dress hanging on the door. Everyone still wants to go. But I can't seem to shake things off so easily.

Rose didn't mention anything about taking Fix tonight. I hope that doesn't come up, since I don't know what I'll do. I'm torn. Nate never shows up anyway. When he does, he doesn't want to talk to me. And I now have more questions for him than ever.

I still have two hours before the dance. I decide to go

to Kmart and find out more about Tabatha. I need closure. I need to know if Nate knew her.

I go to the Kmart and walk up to the service desk. There are a few people in front of me and my nerves are crawling through my skin like some kind of ant farm. I'm not sure what I am going to ask and wonder if I'll even get any information.

After listening to a heavy-set lady complain about finding a smudge on the shirt she bought and discovering that the older man in front of me stood in line just to ask directions to the bathroom, I approach the service desk.

"Hi, I was hoping to talk to a manager or someone who might remember Tabatha Wryter. She was my sister and used to work here."

"What is it you need to know?" the middle-aged woman with long, greasy hair asks me.

"Well, I was hoping to find out who she worked with."

"Sure, let me call the manager for you. Just give me a sec."

After a few minutes, a young man in a red Kmart vest introduces himself to me.

"Hi, I'm Frank. Is there something I can help you with?"

"Yeah, hopefully. Umm, do you remember Tabatha Wryter?"

An expression crosses his face as if he had just seen a ghost.

Cautiously, Frank responds, "Yes, I do. She was a wonderful girl to work with. She got along with everyone here."

"Was she close to anyone?"

"You mean like a boyfriend?" he looks at me puzzled. "We're not supposed to talk about things like that."

"Look, Frank, she was my sister. I hate to be blunt, but she killed herself."

"I know," he says, looking down like he said something wrong. "I'm sorry for your—"

"Yes, thank you," I cut him off, agitated. "My mom mentioned she was close to someone here. Would you happen to know who?"

"Well, come to think of it. There was this one guy. They were pretty friendly with each other. But he was killed soon after your sister passed away."

"He was killed? How? Do you remember his name?"

"Oh, yeah. It's was all over the news, too. He was chasing after some girls or something to the effect and got his foot caught in the railroad tracks. The train came so fast, he died instantly."

"He was chasing some girls? Why?"

"I really don't know the full story. It happened almost a year ago. All I remember was how devastating it was."

"Thank you. If you can remember anything else, here's my number." I write it down on a piece of paper by the service desk, thank him again, and start walking away. As I do, he turns around and stops me.

"Nate!" he calls out. My hair stands on end. "Nate Demarco was his name."

I don't even answer the guy. I just walk in a daze straight out to my car. Then, I sit in the driver's seat and stare at the steering wheel. Numb.

Nate. Why didn't Tabatha ever tell me about him? Was I that wrapped up in my own life, I didn't notice hers?

The railroad tracks. Jenelle used to be bullied by the girls from across the tracks. Was Nate part of the bullying? That's hard to imagine. But, in the Fix circle, he was chasing Candace near railroad tracks.

But the thing that gets me the most: why did Nate appear to me? It seems like it has something to do with Tabatha.

CHAPTER TWENTY-FOUR

Back home, I finish getting ready for the dance. I try to, at least, when all I can think about is Nate and Tabatha and Candace's dead body.

While I look for shoes to wear, my phone jiggles on the dresser. I run to go grab it and see Rose's name light up.

"Hey, you're comin' right?" she asks.

"Yeah, why?"

"Just making sure 'cause of what happened and shit."

I want to ask her why she doesn't really care. I'm about to say something but she cuts me off. "We need to talk."

I'm quiet at first and then tell her, "okay." Maybe she's finally going to tell me why she's being so weird.

We end the call at that. I think about it for a while. I hope this doesn't have anything to do with Clay and the other night.

I rest my phone back on the dresser and go to the mirror to put on mascara.

"Knock, knock," Walker says as he opens the door to my bedroom. He's wearing black jeans and a stylish dark-gray sweater. I slip on the little black party dress that I normally wouldn't be caught dead in. I don't even mind that Walker sees me half-naked. "Your mom just left so I wanted to check on you. Hope that's okay."

"Yeah, it's fine, come in. Can you zip me up?"

He stands behind me and slowly zips up my dress, his

warm hands brushing against my back, and kisses the nape of my neck. "I hope you don't mind that, either."

I turn around and we smile at each other. We've been through so much at this point we really don't say much to each other. We just know. After everything that's happened, our connection has grown deeper than ever. It helps that I am slowly coming to terms with the fact that Nate and I will never be together. I don't know why he came to me in the first place, but I am trying to get over all that now. It's time I quit Fix.

"You look amazing. So, are you ready to go, Pen?"

"Yeah, just let me get my coat. Here." I toss him the keys from my dresser. "You drive tonight." I tell him to warm up the car so I can finish up.

The plan is to meet everyone up at the school by eight o' clock. I'm happy that Jenelle is coming with Jared, too. The table seating is first come, first served and Rose had mentioned that she wanted to get close to the dance floor, so we're leaving early. My nerves amp up as I wonder what Rose wants to talk to me about.

I check one last time in the bathroom mirror to see if I look decent enough and dart downstairs and out the door. We pull out of the driveway, heading down the block onto the main street. It shouldn't take us long to get there. During the car ride we are both silent as we listen to the radio. Walker seems pretty relaxed. I am glad he dropped the whole Clay thing.

I lean my head on the passenger side window as my mind travels back to the Justin incident and how Walker thought we were messing around. Clearly, Walker's changed. Before, he'd go out on a rampage, drinking and getting stoned on Fix. I remember how we'd used to party in some oasis by the expressway and he'd always dodge in between the cars. He was too wild and too hard to get through to back then. Now his entire demeanor has changed.

Last night was a shocker for us all. It put everything into perspective.

We pull into the school parking lot as the senior class gathers at the front entrance. Rose texts me that they are at the corner on the west side of the school. Walking over, I see Rose from afar, waving at us.

"Hey, you! Ready to have some fun?" she yells out. She looks great in her tiny spaghetti-strap dress with black and red flowers on it. It's a Spanish-style gown that totally suits her to a T. "Glad you guys could make it!"

Clay looks at me and turns away. I get the feeling he's ashamed. Rose still doesn't know.

"Pen! Get over here, I want to talk to you," she laughs, urging me off to the side. "Here." She puts something in my hand. "This should help make things a little better tonight."

"Is this why you wanted to talk to me?" I ask her, raising my voice. "Just to ask me to get high with you?"

"Yeah, why not, right?" On the phone, she sounded like it was something serious.

"Take it!"

I look at the tiny round pill and my heart descends into an abyss of worry. What is it going to be like this time? Should I really do this again?

Rose looks at me and waits for me to pop it in my mouth.

"Rose, I don't think it's a good idea . . . not tonight."

"You're gonna take it," she demands. Her face gets hard and her eyes grow wide like she's ready to pounce on me like a jungle cat. The guys are off to the side, talking. "I won't take no for an answer."

I look at Walker, who's having a conversation with Clay. He's going to be upset if I take it. But a part of me still really wants to. I can't help it. Besides, Rose looks like she's going to kill me if I don't. I swallow it instantly. It's only a matter of minutes before everything changes. The usual wave of nausea hits me fast. I start to sweat and feel like I'm turning inside out. The laughing gets louder and travels like a swift flowing current. Everyone's conversation engulfs me with a tidal wave of noise. The mindless chatter seems to have no end.

Inside the school, the music's booming and vibrating off the walls, seeping deep within my brain. The flashing lights flicker, shocking me with electric energy. *And the smells . . . God, the smells.* The baby powder scented deodorant I'm wearing gets clogged in my nose. The sweet aromas of berries and cream and wildflowers from the girls' hair or bodywash overcome me with a head rush. It's like the room is dancing around me. Everywhere I look it's moving in some way.

I try to play it off like nothing bothers me as we sit down at the table closest to the dance floor. Walker is looking at me strangely. Maybe he knows I am high. Inside I am screaming at the top of my lungs, "I'm sorry! Please forgive me!"

Rose takes a seat, while Clay and Walker get us some drinks. That's when Jenelle and Jared come walking up. Rose gives Jenelle a dirty look. But Jenelle shrugs it off and looks away. She rambles on about how happy she is that we all made it. It seems a little fake to me. Maybe she sounds different because I am with my friends—mainly Rose. Maybe it's Fix.

"We're on the other side of the dance floor," Jenelle says.

"So? You must mistake us for people who care." Rose snaps out.

"Rose!" I snap back. "Jenelle, thanks for letting us know."

"Yeah, so, anyway, you guys wanna dance? Jared is going to request some songs. I just love club music," Jenelle says as Rose rolls her eyes.

"Yeah, we do." I tug at Rose's arm. "Don't we, Rose?" She gives me a smartass smile, but agrees anyway. We both get up and walk to the dance floor.

It's crowded already with everyone dancing around us, jumping and waving their hands in the air and everything. Once we all loosen up and let the music move us, everyone seems happy. I glance over at the boys sitting at the table and they seem good, too. Walker holds a glass up, motioning me to come get a drink. I smile and tell him to hold on.

Dancing to the pulsing music and flashing lights, I feel a weird static energy. Looking around the room, people are having a good time. But from across the way, near the punch table, I see a guy with long, dark hair and those unmistakable tattoos.

Dear God, it's Nate.

Suddenly, I have an overwhelming urge to walk over to him. He flashes his silver eyes at me only once and walks away, down the hall.

"Hey, I'm going to head to the bathroom," I tell them.

"What?!" Rose screams. "I can't hear you!"

"The bathroom!" I say louder, pointing to the women's bathrooms.

"Oh, yeah, okay, we'll be right here."

I'm happy to see Rose and Jenelle getting along, dancing together with a few other girls, too. Before I follow Nate, I tell Walker where I'm going, although it's not *really* where I am headed.

I rush down the empty halls, but I don't see anything. Not yet.

"Nate?" I call out softly. I peer into the dark, empty classrooms, but I still don't see him. It isn't until I get to the end of the hall that I hear something.

"Penelope . . ." he calls out.

When I check in the last classroom, I see a dark shadow against the wall. It's him. I know it is. By the dim light streaming in the windows I can see the black symbol etchings on his arms.

"What are you doing here?"

"I came to tell you something," he whispers, stepping out into the light. "Something I should have told you a long time ago."

"Tell me who you are, Nate," I demand, keeping my distance. "Tell me who you *really* are. Are you a . . . ghost?"

"That's what I came here to talk about." He comes closer. I don't ever remember seeing such sadness in his eyes. But they're not silver right now. They're gray and fading, although he still looks beautiful.

I want nothing more than to hold him, to tell him I miss him. But he keeps his distance.

"You may know more than me . . ." his voice trails off. "The life I had before this was only temporary. I have a deeper mission now."

"Tabatha," I bluntly say. "You knew her, didn't you?"

"Yes. She loved you so much. All she really cared about was you."

"Why me, then? Why am I the only one who can see you?"

His eyes twinkle, then start dimming. He looks down for a moment and back into my eyes again. I could cry at how sad he looks.

"I made a promise to her that I'd keep you safe," he tells me.

I hear someone coming and peek out into the hallway. Two security guards walk the halls, flickering their flashlights in each of the empty classrooms.

"But there's more to it," Nate whispers.

I see the lights continue to flash, coming closer.

"Listen, I need to go. I'm going to get caught," I tell him.

"It can't wait any longer, Penelope. I must say this."

More mysteries. I just can't take it.

"Look, can we go somewhere else?" I ask, keeping an eye on the guards.

"No!" He says in a firm voice. "It must be now."

"What's this about, Nate?"

"It's about Tabatha," Nate urges. "You need to know . . ." And just as he's about to tell me, lights float around the room. I don't see him anymore.

"Nate? You there?"

When I turn around, the guards shine their flashlights in my eyes.

"You can't be in here," one of the guards says.

I head out of the room and down the hall, back to the dance, and try to shake off the flutter of excitement within me. I'm glad I finally saw Nate again, but I'm so frustrated that he couldn't finish what he wanted to say. What was it about Tabatha he needed to tell me?

I scan the dance floor to try and find Rose and Jenelle, but they're gone. I go straight to our table and ask Clay where they went. Walker is nowhere to be found either.

"They all went looking for you. Walker thought you guys were all together. He figured you and Rose were getting high, so he went to look, too, just a little while ago," Clay says. "Did you check the bathrooms?"

"No, I'll be right back."

"I'll go look, too."

"Okay then, you check the west side of the school and I'll check the other."

Clay gets up, leaving out of the west side exit. It only takes me a few minutes to check the bathrooms to see they're both not there. My fear rises. The last time someone went missing, it ended horribly.

I don't go straight to security. I probably should, but I'm afraid Rose is getting high somewhere. So, I go alone through the halls, sneaking into the empty classrooms. But I don't see anybody. Clay texts me: **Can't find them.**

My mind is in a whirlwind of fear. I think of Walker. He sure got out of there fast. My thoughts play games with me. Is he involved with this in some way? I don't know what to think.

The halls are quiet in the east wing of the school. Everything is dimly lit. I can't tell what's in each room unless I search them. When I think the fear of the silence has overtaken me, I hear faint muffling noises coming from the auditorium. They echo through the halls.

I slip through the front doors of the auditorium and scan the seating area. Nothing. I walk up the steps of the stage. From the corner of my eye, dark shadows emerge from underneath the curtain.

Is this real? Or is it Fix?

"Rose? Jenelle?" I whisper softly, but no one responds. The muffled noises start up again. My heart is beating so fast, I'm afraid it will stop completely. I don't know what to do. Fear almost sends me running. But I need to find out.

I slowly creep off to the side of the stage and behind the curtain. I swallow my fear and am shocked at what I see.

Rose is tied up in a chair like in a crazy slasher movie. I almost laugh. Is this another prank?

"Mmm, mmm, mmm," Rose muffles underneath the duct tape covering her mouth. She fidgets in the chair, trying to get loose. One look in her terrified eyes, and I know this is for real.

"Rose! Who did this to you?" I ask, trying to peel away the tape.

"Stop what you're doing," a voice says from behind me.

I turn around and see who it is—jade eyes pierce me with a crazy gaze. She's holding a knife in her hand. I cup my mouth and gasp.

"What are you doing, Jenelle?"

"What does it look like?" She slithers out, creeping closer as I step back. "Don't you realize what a bitch Rose is? She needs to be punished!"

"That doesn't mean you have to kill her!"

"You don't know. You don't know what I had to go through. All those times in gymnastics. You are so pathetic, Penelope. It's not even funny."

"Jenelle, just stop this. Talk to me. You don't have to do this." I continue to step back.

"Talk to you? What for? To tell you that Rose and Candace and Kelly were mean bitches that bullied me almost every day of my life? You know all this already. I've tried to tell you so many times and you just blew me off. This has been going on for years. It's time I stop it. All the teasing, pushing, and chasing me after school. It has to come to an end."

"Please stop."

"Stop? Don't you get it?" Her eyes grow wide as her pupils expand. "It had to be done. Kelly was easy. And you guys made it easy to follow Candace after that party. Don't you see, Pen? It was meant to happen."

"You were stalking her the whole time?" I continue to step back as she leans forward. "How could you . . . murder them?"

"Easy. You guys were so stoned you didn't even notice. Nate is gone because of Rose. I can never get him back because of what they did to him."

"Nate?" My blood runs cold. "You . . . you know Nate? What does he have to do with this?"

I keep inching backward. *Does she know that Nate was a real person?*

"Penelope, you're so stupid! Nate wasn't just your imaginary friend. He was my step-brother. You were too high to get that." She snickers a demonic laugh. "Man, it was funny to hear you talk about him. But you wouldn't remember all that, would you?"

Maybe she's right. I don't remember. The drug has killed a lot of my memories.

"After we stopped being friends, they still taunted me," Jenelle continues, holding tight onto the knife, inching closer to me. "He died trying to save me on those railroad tracks that day when they were all chasing me. He was running to save me. God, Penelope, you saw it happen from across the street. It hasn't even been a full year and you don't even remember?"

In shock, I think of the Fix circle. I saw visions of Nate on the tracks. And Candace. I take a deep breath, trying to remember more clearly.

Jenelle smirks and an eerie kindness fills her eyes. "But,

Pen, I'm so glad you're here." She twirls the knife around in her hand. "'Cause this is for you, too."

For a split second, Jenelle looks at Rose. It's my chance to try to lure her away from Rose and somehow get help. I dart behind the curtain and run up the steps to the catwalk to hide.

"Where are you Penelope?" Jenelle yells out as her voice echoes off the walls. "Show yourself!"

I shudder. This is some seriously crazy shit. She looks around and spots me on the catwalk and races up the steps. I try to make my way down again, but she catches me at the very end of the landing.

"You really are that stupid, aren't you?" Jenelle spits out, rubbing the knife along her thigh. Blood pools out, staining her dress.

"Jenelle, just stop now while you have the chance."

As I hold my hands up again, she gives me an evil stare and lunges. I grab hold of her wrist as the two of us struggle to control the knife. She shoves me on one side as I shove her on the other. With all my might, I squeeze her wrist, forcing her to drop the knife.

"You bitch!" she yells, grabbing for the knife again as I kick it out of the way. Again, she lunges, but this time I crouch down and duck out of the way. Her body flips over the edge of the catwalk, but she grips tightly to the ropes over the stage several feet below.

I cower backward, but my heart pulls at me. I can't just leave Jenelle hanging there. "Here! Take my hand," I tell her, stretching my hand out as far down as I can. Slowly, she crawls up the ropes, reaching for me. For a moment, I look at her and see the fear in her eyes. "Come on, Jenelle, reach!"

She grabs the ropes as high as she can and extends her arm out one more time. But it's the last time. Her grasp slips, and she plummets seventy-five feet down onto the stage below.

Detectives Reeves and Wesson gather all the students in empty classrooms throughout the school for questioning. In the auditorium, there's a flock of kids at the corner by the doors all crying and staring at Jenelle's dead body. She lays all broken and twisted on center stage while the forensic team take pictures and put markers around the blood splatters. Two burly police officers tape off the whole section of the stage.

I'm trying to take it all in. I never would have suspected that Jenelle would do anything like this. I remind myself of what she said moments before she fell, about how she was following Candace during the party. She was planning this the whole time. Maybe Justin did walk Candace halfway home. That's probably when Jenelle got to her.

Walker runs up to me, "Are you okay?"

"Yeah, where were you?"

"Looking for you." He takes me in his arms and we embrace.

I look around the room and see Rose wrapped in a thick wool blanket, shivering as she talks to one of the police officers. After he hands her a cup of water and leaves, I see Candace's charm bracelet dangling from her wrist. If she didn't have anything to do with this, how did she get Candace's bracelet? How does she feel knowing that Jenelle wanted to kill her? Releasing myself from Walker's arms, I tell him I'll be right back and walk over to Rose.

"So, you all right?" I ask Rose as she sips the water.

"Yeah, just really shook up." I take another look at her wrist and blurt out. "Hey, isn't that Candace's bracelet?"

"I don't know. Is it?" she says before swallowing another sip. "It was on the floor in my basement, during the Fix party. I figured someone left it there." She looks at me. She's still in shock, her eyes bulging in the light as she stares blankly. "She was there that night, wasn't she?"

"You mean Jenelle?"

"Yeah, I remember now. I thought I saw her a few times during the party, wearing a dark, hooded parka. It was creepin' me out. I thought I was seeing things from the high. I never invited her. And a few nights after, I could have sworn I saw her across the street, with that same dark parka on, just staring into my front window."

"Why didn't you mention this before?"

"Like I said, I thought it was from Fix. Man, Pen, I was so stoned out of my mind, during the circle and all those other times. I'm surprised I even remember it now."

She takes another sip and shivers again, evidently thinking of what she just said.

"Pen?" Rose whispers, looking up at me.

"Yeah, what is it?"

"About the Fix circle. There's something I need to tell you."

I look at her. "Yes?"

"It was my idea to scare you guys during the circle. I soaked your pills in cough syrup. It messed with your high."

"God, Rose! Why?"

178

"I was just trying to have a little fun. I didn't know you and Walker would get so messed up. The guys and I were in the hooded robes. We didn't hurt Nate or anything. I swear." She bends her head down. "Maybe we took it too far. Maybe I took a lot of things too far—like messin' with Jenelle. It finally backfired on me." Guilt overcomes her as tears well up in her eyes.

"Look, Rose. We all make mistakes, but no one deserves to get murdered over it. C'mon."

She looks down, holding the cup to her lips and staring back into the crowd. She seems to ponder the entire ordeal and struggles to accept my answer, yet she mumbles out, "Yeah, you're right. Thanks for not freaking out over what I did that night."

I could lash out and scream at her over what she put me and Walker through during that weird trip, but why bother? It's not important anymore.

Just then an overwhelming wave of nausea rumbles within my stomach and starts to travel up into my throat. I realize the effects from Fix are wearing off. The room spins as I try to balance myself. I look around, trying to focus, but it's too hard. Struggling with my stomach issues, I glance toward the far end of the room and see him . . . again. Dark etchings creep out of his plain white shirt and down his arm. He looks different, more natural this time, like he could be one of the students, yet it's definitely him.

Nate, why am I still seeing you?

He turns around and looks me dead in the face with those same familiar, silver eyes. A shock of fear jolts through me. I thought I saw him that one time, at the bus stop, but I convinced myself it wasn't him, because I wasn't high. But now? It can't be true. *Can it?* My mind is playing tricks on me. It has to be.

I look down and take a few deep breaths, hoping to clear my mind—hoping to make these feelings go away. I dare myself to look again. He's gone. I sigh in relief.

"I'm so glad you're okay, Pen." I startle, but it's Walker's voice, not Nate's. Walker wraps his arms around me.

"Yeah, me, too," I mumble in his ear, nestling my face close to his.

"Yeah, well the worst is over now. You're safe," he whispers.

I don't say anything. We just hold each other. All I can think of is: why am I still seeing Nate? And what was it he had to tell me about Tabatha? I have a sick feeling my troubles are not over yet.

CHAPTER TWENTY-SIX

It's been a rough few days talking to the police. Their interrogation is making me feel guilty that I didn't pick up on things sooner. So many times, I heard Detective Reeves say, "If you weren't so high all the time, you'd remember." The phrase plays over and over in my mind as I pace around the house.

And I guess I knew Nate when he was alive. I'd at least met him before. I just don't remember. Maybe I saw him when Jenelle and I were kids. And Jenelle . . . I still can't get that image out of my mind, her broken and bloody body lying on the stage.

All day long I've been trying to sleep things off. My nightmares are getting more horrific by the day. Strange dreams of Tabatha invade my nights. On top of it all, my mom has been ignoring me. After the Ken incident, she's been acting like she's in a catatonic state. I don't know what she's thinking. I can't take it anymore. I've sunk lower than the ocean floor, and I'm anchored to my thoughts.

I want to get so high that I never snap out of it. There are three pills left in Tabatha's jewelry box. I decide I'm going to take all of them to erase everything—the murders, this mess with my mom, and the ghostly hallucinations of Nate. It's time to end everything once and for all. I don't know what Nate's trying to tell me. I don't know if I ever will. I want this confusion between my real-life torments and hallucinations to end.

In the spare bedroom by the kitchen, I draw the blinds and lock the doors. My mom is at work and I'm alone. I don't even bother with a good-bye note because I doubt it if she'd even care. Walker will just have to understand. When you are living between a dream and reality, to me, it's a living hell. And I don't want to live in this darkness anymore.

I take the pills out of my top drawer and watch them roll around in my hand before I sit on the bed. One window blind is open a crack, which I am too lazy to get up and close. The dim orange light of the setting sun peeks through the slits. Grabbing the bottle of water from my nightstand, I shove the pills in my mouth. With one big gulp, I wash them down. The room starts spinning as I hear a faint knocking. *Is it coming from inside the walls?* I'm not sure. I can't tell if it's somewhere from inside the house or just in my head.

I curl myself up in a fetal position. The knocking is getting louder, so loud my head's pounding. I close my eyes and flashes of the scene at school flicker in my mind. Jenelle's dead body mutates into Candace's dead body in the woods. And they still haven't found Kelly's body yet. But in my mind, she's lying in the woods, too. All these dead bodies start piling up in my head. I am covered in them. The walls begin to close in on me. I'm trapped in a box. I pound on the boards to get out. And that knocking continues. Between that knocking and my banging on the wood, everything gets numbingly loud until it all stops. I blank out.

I wake up in a white room. With blurred vision, I see someone sitting next to me.

"Hey, honey, you're awake." It's my mom's voice. As my

eyes slowly focus, I see her with hair pulled back and eyes sunken in. She looks like she hasn't slept in days.

"How did I get here?" I say in a raspy voice.

"Walker," my mom says.

"Huh?"

"If it wasn't for Walker breaking in, you wouldn't be here."

"What?" I sit up, looking down at the IV inserted in my arm.

"They had to pump your stomach. Walker saw you from the side window slumped over on the bed, so he broke the window to get in." She looks at me with concerned eyes. "You tried to OD, Penelope. Why?"

"I don't know. I just felt so alone."

"You could have just come to me. I love you so much, Penelope." She squeezes my hand and smiles, but I pull my hand away.

"What about Ken?"

"What about Ken? He's gone."

"For good?"

"No one treats my daughter like that. I'm sorry it took me so long to realize you needed me."

She gives me a tight embrace and sobs softly on my shoulder.

"I'm mad at myself for allowing this to happen. It's my fault. I should have been a better mother. I'm so sorry, Penelope. Never again. I'm here for you always."

After being released from the hospital, my mom and I talked about everything I could think of. We both agreed that I need to get help. I'm sad I'll never see Nate again, but I must get help. It's the only way.

My mom arranged for me to go to rehab at the Winston Center for Drug and Alcohol Addiction for Young Girls. I agreed, as long as I stay there for only two weeks and participate in out-patient therapy afterward. I don't want to miss any more school.

I pack my things as we get ready to drive the two hours downstate to the center. I'm still having stomach pains and monster headaches, and since my mood swings haven't been all that great, the doctor has put me on a mood stabilizer. After the doctor explained I may be suffering from depression, he put me on something for that, too. All this and I have to go through rehab.

"Pen, are you ready?" my mom yells from downstairs.

"Yeah, just a minute," I yell back, looking around the room one last time. I notice my phone sitting on the top shelf of my bookcase. I'm dreading that I won't be able to use it for the next two weeks. I stall for a few more minutes, hoping that Walker will call. But nothing. I'm unsure of how our relationship is going. I was hoping he'd say good-bye before I left. Guess that's not going to happen.

I inhale a deep breath, thinking of what I have ahead of me. It sucks that I have to go, but I am ready to move forward with my life. I'm trying to stay confident that this treatment will work for me. Hoping is more like it. After everything that's happened, my nightmares still haunt me. Lately, I've been having dreams of Tabatha where she's standing by a creek in the woods, lost and crying. I still feel like there's something she wants to tell me.

Finally, I close the door to my room and head downstairs.

From the driveway, mom honks the horn. I hesitate, thinking I'll hear my phone ring from upstairs—hoping that Walker hasn't forgotten about me leaving today, but all I hear is silence.

We pull up at the Winston Center a little after five. After my mom parks the car, she asks me again how I'm feeling.

"Just tired," I tell her, dragging myself out of the car. She opens the trunk and reaches to grab for my things. She looks like she's ready to cry, but holds in her sniffles and just smiles at me.

As the automatic doors open with a *swoosh*, she grabs my hand and tells me she loves me. The patterned carpet in the lobby makes me feel dizzy. I can only imagine how my mother is feeling, knowing her second daughter was on the same drug that killed her firstborn. I never meant for things to turn out this way. And I'm anxious about what's going to happen to me. The counselor explained the twelve-step program, and I groaned at the thought of "letting God into my life." I was never a religious person, and I'm not about to start now. But if it's going to help me get better, I am willing to try it.

We sign in at the reception desk and wait for Mrs. Pendergast, the director of the drug and alcohol program, to come in and give us a tour. She introduces herself and leads us into a big, open room where a few young girls are sitting by the TV. There are a few other girls playing cards at a table by the huge glass windows like everything is fine. I wonder what got them here. Was it drugs or alcohol? Did they take Fix like me?

"This is our dayroom," she says. "Many recreational activities take place here. I think you'll like it here, Penelope."

She guides us down a long, narrow hallway, brightly lit from the sun, and shows us the cafeteria. It doesn't seem so bad. It reminds me of the food court at the mall, with its round tables and thin metal chairs. It even has a high ceiling with windows. At least I can see the sky from here.

"Let me show you something that I think you'll enjoy, Penelope," Mrs. Pendergast says as she catches me staring up into the sky. She takes us to the east wing of the building and into a beautiful atrium filled with lush, green plants and sweet-smelling flowers. There are a few seating areas to perhaps read or just gaze out the windows. I'm guessing all patients must stay inside, so this is the closest I'll get to the outside world.

I catch sight of a silvery ball of light. It startles me at first as I watch it glint across the room. Instantly, I think of Nate and his silver eyes. I watch it dance on the wall and shoot out the window. I take a deep breath, thinking maybe there's still a chance I'll see him. *Could it even be possible?*

"And where will she be staying?" my mom asks, snapping me back into reality.

"Oh, here, let me show you. This way."

We head back toward the cafeteria. Mrs. Pendergast points to the right, down a long hall. My room is at the end, she tells me. Anxiety starts to rise within me like I'm slowly going up a roller coaster. When I finally stand in the doorway, looking around the room, my heart stops dropping. It's not that bad. The walls are painted a soft cream color, and a huge glass-block window takes up most of the far wall of the room. There are two twin-sized beds, one on each side. But I still feel trapped.

"You'll see that this room gets a lot of light in the morning and afternoon. And as far as I know, you'll have it all to yourself for the next two weeks," Mrs. Pendergast says with a smile.

"Well, I guess I better be going," my mom says. "I'll get your things from the front desk."

"Good, I'll leave you two alone for a while. If you need anything as you're getting settled in, I'll be here all day. The nursing staff is here 24/7."

"Thank you," my mom says, just before she leaves to go to the front desk.

I sit down and feel my eyelids getting heavy, so I lay down, curling up in a ball. A flood of energy fills me at the thought Nate may come back to me. But I don't want to get my hopes up.

My mom returns and sets my things on a chair in the corner.

"Good, rest. You need that," she says as she strokes my hair. "You know you can call me any time you want." Even though I can't use my cell phone or a computer at all, the staff explained to us that I can use the public phones from as early as six in the morning until as late as ten at night.

"I'll leave you to get acclimated. I'll be back later in the week." She kisses me good-bye with tears in her eyes and heads out.

I continue to lie on the bed, trying to soak everything in. I'm scared and lonely and aggravated and feel like I can barely contain my anger. But I know this is the best thing for me right now.

I close my eyes and try to concentrate on how good it will be to get out of here and feel better. Even though I haven't begun detox yet, I am determined to make things work.

Lying there, I think of all the things that have recently happened.

Tabatha. She suddenly floods my mind. Nate never did get a chance to tell me everything.

Images of Tabatha getting ready for work come into my mind. She looks as beautiful as ever, even in her uniform. With her golden hair twisted in a half-ponytail, half-bun, she's brushing mascara on her eyelashes. She always wore very little makeup. She never needed anything more than that and a little lip gloss. As I picture her walking out the door and into the bright light, I fall into a deep sleep.

Imagines of Tabatha in the forest flash before me. She's waiting by the creek near the old railroad tracks. I see her poking the ground with a stick. She keeps checking her watch as she waits for something or someone. Then suddenly someone does come. He is standing behind her. When she turns around, she faces him and at first, she's happy, putting her arms around him and smiling. I can't make out who he is. I just see the back of his head: long, dark hair. She looks at him intently and starts to shake her head "no." Tears stream down her face as she cups her hands over her cheeks. She is so sad, but why?

He mumbles something to her as she cries and shakes her head. He is telling her something, something bad. She gets mad and slaps him. His head swivels to the side in slow motion. I get a good look at him. That same chiseled face and those unmistakable silver eyes. I hear her calling his name. *Nate!* He starts walking away—toward me, as if I was standing right there, but I'm not. I'm nothing but the thin, cold air that hangs over them. He's leaving her. As everything turns black all around her, she looks up into the dark sky and cries out one final scream, so piercing I jolt and wake up.

I manage to tough it out for my first full week here, but it's hard. Even though I have people to talk to, I keep to myself. No more sightings of anything unusual, unfortunately. Now that I'm thinking with a clear mind, I'm really starting to miss Walker. I keep asking my mom if she's heard anything, but she hasn't. With each passing day, I fear that he's forgotten about me. That he changed his mind.

I picture him moving on with his life. It seemed so easy for him to quit Fix. And here I am locked up in this place, sometimes feeling worse than before. I can't seem to shake the Tabatha nightmares. I don't know why, after all these months, that I am having them now. Maybe it's because I am officially off the drug. Or maybe she's trying to tell me something in her own way.

"Okay, ladies, the first morning meeting is about to start, please join us in the dayroom," Mrs. Pendergast says to all of us. Breakfast is just about done and everyone gets up to stack their dirty trays on the cart.

I stare into my soupy scrambled eggs and half-empty glass of orange juice, hoping my mother will call soon. I sit there enjoying the silence. It has become so quiet that I can hear the wall clock ticking.

As I get up to put my tray away, I hear something from down the hall. I find it strange since everyone is at the other end in the dayroom. I go down the hall to check out the noise. The slick, shiny reflection of the floor reflects someone walking down the hall and to the atrium.

The figure looks so familiar that I am compelled to follow it.

A surge of energy zips around inside me, like I'm on the edge of hearing good news—something that's going to make me feel better in some way. *Nate?*

I follow the figure down a winding path of flowers and thick plants. If I can just get around the corner, I can find out who it is.

I walk around the cemented path, feeling a slight chill in the air. There's a soft breeze ruffling the tall palm trees overhead and their fronds flutter in the wind. I wonder where the cold draft is coming from.

"Penelope," someone calls out.

Turning the corner, I stop in shock. My whole body stiffens in fear. A young man is standing by the edge of the pond, his back turned. He has that familiar dark hair and build. Just like in my dreams.

"Nate? Is that you?"

The young man turns around. My heart sinks when I see it's just a staff member. "The meeting has started. Please go to the dayroom," he tells me.

"Yes, umm, sorry. I'm on my way." I turn to make my way to the dayroom, afraid to turn back toward the pond, but I will myself to do so. Slowly peering over my shoulder, behind me all I see are purple and pink flowers, their heavy blooms drooping above the pond.

We form a circle in the dayroom and recite the serenity prayer. After we're through, everyone takes their seats. Mrs. Pendergast begins with an introduction. Even though we all know each other by now, she insists that we start by introducing ourselves and telling the group what our addiction is. The tall, thin girl across from me starts.

"Hi, I'm Christina. But as you guys all know, you can just call me Chris." She pauses with a laugh. "I am addicted to methamphetamines. But my friends and I call it Tik. Well, they used to be my friends. Now, I don't know." She fidgets in her seat, twirling her hair around her fingers.

"Tell us how you're feeling today, Chris," Mrs. Pendergast says.

Chris goes into how lonely she feels and how her depression is starting to overpower her. Oddly enough, it intrigues me. Not that I am glad to hear she's depressed, but that I am not alone in how I feel. Many of the girls are the same way. Six out of the twelve here, including me, are addicted to Fix.

Each one of us mentions the same symptoms of withdrawal. It really doesn't matter what kind of addiction you have, it all results in depression.

Mrs. Pendergast explains how these drugs work and their effects on users. She mentions a few things about Fix that catch my attention.

"As you know, Fix, LSD, and even marijuana can make you hallucinate. Many hallucinogens affect thought patterns, the perception in your way of thinking, they change your emotional state and consciousness. Many patients going through withdrawal suffer through these changes. These types of experiences often spur on abnormal thinking and dream patterns, in many cases, nightmares and night tremors."

I can't help but think of the weird dreams I've been having about Tabatha. It all seems to make sense now, that I would be experiencing these things.

"Thankfully, these side effects subside as you continue treatment. The medication you've been prescribed should help quell that. Remember to give your body time to get used to the new medication. Many people that are in denial of their illness stop taking their meds and relapse."

My mind snags on the word "illness." I never realized it before, but this is what it really is. I have to continually admit that I have an illness and it's not going to go away in a day. I know it's going to take time. And I know each day is going to be a battle. Hopefully, from this point, things will get better.

After dinner, everyone has some free time before visiting hours begin. My mom called earlier, letting me know she'll be up to see me. She mentioned she has something for me.

I decide to return to the pond in the atrium. Running my fingers through the water, I can't help but think Nate is still with me. I want him to be. In my heart, I know he was trying to tell me something. I wonder how much more of this I can take. Will I keep seeing Nate for the rest of my life? I remember what Mrs. Pendergast said at the meeting earlier. My adverse side effects should subside over time.

But even then, I will struggle. I worry that I'll always be tormented by Tabatha's death. If I just knew why she decided to kill herself, I think I could cope. But I'll never know.

"Hey, I was looking all over for you," my mom says. "Should we stay here, or go in your room?"

"Here's fine."

"How are you?"

"Could be better, could be worse," I laugh.

"Are they treating you okay?" She takes a seat beside me.

"Yeah, it's okay here."

"Well, you don't have much more to go. Another week and you'll be out of here."

I think of the time I've taken off school and wonder how it's going to be catching up. Sure, I'll be out of this place, but I have a long road ahead.

"I have something for you." She rummages through her purse and pulls out an envelope. "It's from Walker."

My heart springs up when she says his name. I take the envelope and thank her, and ask if he's said anything more.

"No," she says. "He seemed to be in a rush. Would you like to read it now? I can go get a cup of coffee or something?"

"Sure, I'd like that."

She gives me another smile before she gets up to leave. "Be right back."

I take a few seconds to examine the envelope. He has handwritten my name, "Penelope," in bold, black ink. I take a deep breath and open it.

Dear Penelope,

Sorry I haven't been around lately. I wanted to say good-bye. I really did. I just couldn't. Things have been difficult, Pen. Even though I've been sober for 21 days, it's still difficult. I've had some time to think. All these years we've known each other. I needed you. Even breaking up those few times. But this? This has been the longest I've been away from you. I miss you, Pen. I can't stop thinking about that night, when we first started taking Fix at the Tower. I pushed you away. I'm sorry for that, too. I feel like this is all my fault. I should have protected you. I know you blame your sister's suicide for pushing you over the edge. But I should have known better, too. You're so beautiful to me, Pen. I don't ever want to ruin that. So many times, I thought we'd always be together—have kids and a white picket fence and all that. But when we broke up last year, I felt like all that was gone.

Now after everything, I still hope we have a chance.

I love you, Penelope.

Hope to see you soon.

Love,

Walker

For the first time in a long time, I feel Walker is finally his true self. The young boy I fell in love with years ago has grown up and become a man. So many times I've wished for this but doubted it. Reading his words gives me hope that Walker and I will make it through this.

CHAPTER TWENTY-EIGHT

It's my last day at the Winston Center and even though I am still having nightmares about Tabatha, I'm learning more about Fix and finding ways to cope. I started a journal a few days ago, tracking my memories of Tabatha and writing about my relationship with Walker and the recent incidents that have transpired.

Waiting for my mom in the atrium, the golden afternoon sunlight warms me and I find a real sense of peacefulness around such beauty. In my own funny way, I feel like I'm in heaven. I sort of wish I was. I could ask Tabatha why she left me.

Mrs. Pendergast says there are many phases of grief, and anger is one of them. She said if I can try to get past it, things will get a little easier over time. I think if my mom and I talk about her more—keep her spirit alive somehow—maybe things will get better.

I check the clock mounted on the wall to see what time it is. Mom should be here soon. I have everything packed, have ten tons of paperwork on how to get better and information on the drugs I'm taking to go through, and all I need now is my mother's signature on the discharge forms and I'll be out of here.

I continue to write my thoughts down, remembering that night at the Tower when I first took Fix, when I first met Nate.

Oh, Nate, how I've missed you so. I am forever grateful for the things you've done for me.

Looking up, I see a flutter of light float across the room. It dances in the air and kisses all the flowers with its touch, and zooms around the corner. I feel a familiar rush of energy. It's the same feeling of excitement that I had when I was with Nate. Something inside urges me to follow it. I set my notebook down and set off around the corner. Warm sunlight drenches my face with its rays. I squint my eyes for a moment or two and see the dancing ball of light transform into a translucent figure. His dark hair waves around his head as if he was under water. His eyes, once silver, are now like two small mirrors. I see my reflection in his eyes.

"Nate?" I whisper softly.

"This is the last time you'll see me," he whispers back.

He's like a blur, the light is bright and magnificent. I want to move closer, but he's emanating so much heat that a bead of sweat streams down my left temple.

"You're healing nicely," he says with a smile. "I'm so proud of you, Penelope."

"Why did you come back to me Nate?"

"There's something that needs to be said."

"What is it?" I shield my eyes from the blinding light.

"It's about Tabatha," he pauses. "Me and Tabatha."

I nod. I'm ready for this now.

"We secretly dated. I was so in love with her. But it was my fault . . ." his voice trails off.

I feel just a slight twist of jealousy in my stomach. They were a couple. But I know that it's never really been romantic between Nate and I. And what I really want now is answers.

"It was my fault," he repeats. "She killed herself because of me, Penelope."

"Wha- What do you mean?"

"You need to know," he pauses again. "Tabatha needs you to know."

"Why couldn't she come to me herself then? Why you?"

"Because her spirit has moved on. My fate was different. It was my duty to protect you. I gave Kelly and Candace's spirits access to you to warn you. To keep you safe from Jenelle."

I shiver. It wasn't just Fix. I really did see Kelly and Candace.

"Is that it?"

Nate shrinks back, shaking his head. "I'll never able to forgive myself for what happened in the woods with Tabatha that day. I broke up with her. I broke up with her when she told me—"

"When she told you what? Nate? Please, come out with it already."

"When she told me she was pregnant."

"What? She was pregnant?"

Nate nods.

I stare in disbelief.

As I try to absorb his words, all the blood rushes to my head and the room suddenly begins to spin. Everything in my mind presses together, it's hard to breathe. The flutter of light hovers in front of me for a quick moment then leaves through the window. I hear Nate say his final words, "Good-bye, Penelope. I hope someday you'll be able to forgive me."

My body descends into a freefall. I can't control the urge to tumble into the darkness. With every inch of me

I try to fight it. But I can't. Like the flick of a light switch, everything goes black.

"Penelope? Wake up." I hear my mother's voice say. "Please, Pen."

I open my eyes and see a few nurses on staff along with my mom standing over me.

"You just fainted, sweetie," the tall red-headed nurse says. "It was probably due to the medication."

I sit up, trying to remember what had just happened. My mind is invaded by Nate's words. Tabatha killed herself. Over him.

"You'll be all right, honey. You can rest on the car ride home."

One of the nurses and my mom guide me to the front desk. After my mom signs me out, we leave, walking through the parking lot to the car and head home.

CHAPTER TWENTY-NINE

I've been clean and sober for six weeks. The last drug test I had showed that Fix is now officially out of my system.

During the car ride when I first came home my mom and I talked—really talked. We got into it about Tabatha and she confessed that she knew Tabatha had been pregnant because of the autopsy report. At first I was livid with my mom, giving her the silent treatment for a whole week. But somehow, I understood why she didn't tell me. After discussing things further, I believed her when she said she didn't know anything about Tabatha and Nate being together. She didn't want to upset me any more than I already was. And thankfully, I haven't had any nightmares since I got home.

When I got back, the school was still buzzing about the Jenelle incident. The police found Kelly's body a few weeks ago, not too far away from where Candace was found. All that time, and I never imagined Jenelle would do anything like this. I guess the bullying really messed her up.

"Pen, Walker's here for you," my mom says from the bottom of the stairwell.

"Okay, be right there."

My mom has officially stopped seeing Ken. I think me being in rehab put things into perspective for her. We have grown closer since then and things have gotten so much better. Even though I have been clean for more than a month, I am still getting nosebleeds and nausea. I went to the doctor last week for more testing and found out that I have clinical depression—like Tabatha. I have to continue taking medication, probably for the rest of my life. Though I am happy that my side effects have subsided a great deal, I fear I might be gaining new ones like dizziness and headaches.

"Knock, knock, you ready to go?" Walker says, standing in my bedroom doorway.

"Yeah, just a minute."

I go to Tabatha's room to grab her urn. Today is the one-year anniversary of Tabatha's death. The plan is to go to the Tower and spread her ashes there. All my pain stemmed from that very spot. I thought it would be fitting to finally let go of Tabatha there. It's also a good place—the place I found Nate. He was a spirit from Tabatha's past, only trying to protect me. Maybe somehow, they can find each other again.

I double-check my bag, making sure I have everything, and head out with Walker to drive downtown.

At the Tower, we meet up with the landlord, taking the elevator this time. I want to get in and out and not screw around anymore. I'm going through a lot of therapy and doing other things to try to cope with my addiction. But I'll admit, it's hard seeing this place again. It makes me think of Rose. She still uses. I don't want to tempt myself, so we don't hang out. We wave to each other in the halls at school every now and then, but that's it. I promised Walker I would stay away from that crowd. I don't want to ever get caught up in it again.

We get to the top and walk over to the gated area. The

landlord unlocks it and tells us to only take a few minutes. We promise him it won't take long and head upstairs.

It's windy and overcast as usual, but I know this is something I have to do. Walker looks at me and tells me this is for the best and I agree. Before we left he suggested that I write a letter to Tabatha including all the things I've always wanted to say to her and burn it on the rooftop.

I take the letter out of my pocket and flick the lighter underneath it, watching the flame eat up the paper. As thin bits of blackened sheets float away, I think of what I wrote. I promised her I will never get high again and that I will take care of myself. I wrote that I've finally forgiven Nate for what happened. For weeks, I examined my relationship with Nate. Bits of images spark in my mind. It was really just a friendship-type of love. Thinking about it now, it feels like one big dream. Nate following me everywhere I went, always keeping me safe. My life was a crazy, beautiful madness of color and heat and light when I was with Nate. It was as if I was in a strange vortex that felt like a brief moment in time, yet lasted a year. But it wasn't safe. It was a year of my life wasted on Fix.

As I stand here looking out into the distance, my mind rewinds to what I've learned in the past few weeks. I'd go to the park or near the school grounds and experience these bits of messages flashing through my thoughts. Nate got Tabatha pregnant, and instead of helping her, he turned her away. He failed her.

But we all make mistakes. I know in my heart, he didn't mean to hurt her. With each passing day, I have come to accept it and move on.

Walker hands me Tabatha's urn. I take it from him and

pour the ashes into the wind. He holds my hand and smiles. I know we will be together for the long haul this time. He really is good to me. And if we are both open and honest with each other, our relationship will only get better.

Walker and I empty out the last of Tabatha's ashes. The clouds separate and the sky begins to clear, letting in amazing light. The setting sun peers out between the buildings and it feels like I'm right inside the purple sky. And if I look hard enough, I can see a thin cloud of pink on the horizon. Finally, for the first time in my life, I know things will be alright.

ACKNOWLEDGMENTS

Thank you to Flux for giving me this amazing opportunity. Special thanks to my editor, Mari Kesselring, for picking my novel out of the slush pile and bringing it to life. Mari, you've always been so encouraging throughout this process and a great joy to work with, thank you.

I would like to thank my husband, Michael. Thank you for being my consultant and helping me figure out what to do always. And for listening to my writing woes! Thank you to my glorious daughter, Abigail Rayanne for the kindest and sweetest support. You've always made Mama feel so much better. And you're right, I shouldn't worry so much. Thank you to my marvelous son, Jake Anthony. Thank you for giving me such great advice and helping me stay motivated with my writing. I will always love your ideas.

And a big shout-out to my online writing community, Absolute Write. Thank you everyone for your critical eye and much needed author support.

ABOUT THE AUTHOR

Lisa M. Cronkhite is the author of *Dreaming a Reality*, *Demon Girl*, *Deep in the Meadows*, and *Disconnected*. Her work has also appeared online and in print magazines including *Storyteller*, *Poetry Salzburg Review*, and *Ruminate Magazine*. She lives and writes in a small suburb near Chicago. You can find her online at www.writingsbylisamcronkhite.blogspot.com and on Twitter @lmcronkhite.